W0246902

PENGUIN METRO READS
SHE FRIEND-ZONED MY LOVE

Sudeep Nagarkar is the author of nine bestselling novels. A recipient of the Youth Achievers' Award, he has also been featured on the *Forbes India* longlist of the most influential celebrities for three consecutive years. He has given guest lectures at renowned institutes like the IITs and organizations like TEDx. His books have been translated into various languages including Hindi, Marathi and Telugu.

Sudeep lives in Mumbai. *She Friend-Zoned My Love* is his tenth book.

Connect with Sudeep via his:
Facebook fan page: /sudeepnagarkar
Facebook profile: /nagarkarsudeep
Twitter: sudeep_nagarkar
Instagram: sudeepnagarkar

Sudeep Nagarkar

She Friend-Zoned My Love

Penguin
metro reads

An imprint of Penguin Random House

PENGUIN METRO READS

USA | Canada | UK | Ireland | Australia
New Zealand | India | South Africa | China | Singapore

Penguin Metro Reads is part of the Penguin Random House group of companies
whose addresses can be found at global.penguinrandomhouse.com

Published by Penguin Random House India Pvt. Ltd
4th Floor, Capital Tower 1, MG Road,
Gurugram 122 002, Haryana, India

First published in Penguin Metro Reads by Penguin Random House India 2018

10 9 8 7 6 5 4 3 2

ISBN 9789385990007

Typeset in Sabon by Manipal Digital Systems, Manipal

Printed at Repro India Limited

www.penguin.co.in

*To all those who get trapped in
the 'just friends' zone*

Contents

Contents

Prologue

When your love is on the line, it's not unusual to wake up with an aching heart, your head full of both pleasant and unpleasant memories. Apurv's mornings had followed a similar pattern ever since his love had left him. Even though he had fallen head over heels for her, she didn't think of him as anything more than a friend.

There's nothing like love, the rousing feeling of first love, he often thought during their initial interactions.

He had had his eyes on countless girls before he met her. Desperate to get into a relationship since his high-school days, he had spent hours on Facebook scrolling through their social media profiles. He even stood in front of their houses, just to catch a glimpse of them. This had continued when he joined junior college earlier this year. However, despite his consistent attempts, nothing seemed to make a difference and tubes of Fair & Handsome went to waste.

A dejected-looking Apurv was chatting on the phone with his best friend Sia.

'You are acting like last night wasn't good enough.'

'Please stop it.'

'Do you want me to sympathize? I am your best friend. It doesn't come naturally to me.'

Even though Apurv was clearly stressed, she continued to mock him relentlessly.

'It's been two weeks, three days and fourteen hours,' he murmured.

This obsessive attention to the time since their last call was because she had mysteriously disappeared after hanging up. It was around eleven at night when Apurv received a call from her asking him to pick her up. Although he had no clue of her whereabouts, he had sneaked out of his house on his Vespa without thinking twice.

'Where are you? I have just arrived,' he had said on the phone on reaching the location she had mentioned. Parking his Vespa on the side stand and taking off his helmet, he sat on the seat scanning the area.

'I am not 100 per cent sure but I think I am at the Andheri bus depot.'

Her response had confused Apurv because he was at the same location. Shortly after that, she had told Apurv that her phone battery was low, and before Apurv could receive her location on WhatsApp, her phone died. After the bizarre phone call, he had driven around the area, showing her picture to passers-by, asking if they had seen anyone like her. She had told him where she was moments ago, and then she had simply vanished. Since this incident, no one had seen her. Phone calls went unanswered and she stopped coming to college. Her voice remained etched in his memory and he often replayed their last discussion in his mind.

It was one of those muggy days when the stars were in hiding, blanketed by the thick city smog. Apurv sat in the corner of his dimly lit room, thinking about her smile. The broken lamp, the dying bulb that flickered hopelessly, the torn photographs and the empty glass of beer were all witness to his heartbreak.

'Your mind seems to be paralysed. We haven't done anything apart from discuss her for the past few days. You should get a life,' Sia said as she tried hanging up on him. His constant cribbing was getting on her nerves.

'It wouldn't have mattered this much if she kept attending classes regularly. What frustrates me is that none of the shopkeepers near her house recall seeing her ever.'

'She vanished faster than a Bollywood star kid's acting career. No, faster than a married man on discovering his secretary's pregnancy test results.'

'This is not a joke. Who was she and what was the purpose of her lies? After speaking to the shopkeepers, I decided to knock on her door and see for myself. I knew exactly where she lived because I had dropped her home once. But even her address turned out to be false. She never lived there. The man who opened the door thought I was trying my luck on his daughter and kicked me out.'

'Apurv, you are stressing yourself out unnecessarily. Everything will return to normal with time. I understand that you are going through a rough patch but overthinking will only make it worse.'

'Do you think she did it intentionally?'

'Only she can answer that question. I don't understand why this is affecting you so much. As far as I know, she was not your girlfriend. I know you had feelings for her but she never treated you as anything more than a friend. Then why are you still stuck on her?'

'She was not just a friend.'

'Whatever.'

'Was she conning me?'

'No. She was a mistake. Get over it.'

'I don't want to feel like a loser again,' Apurv was dejected.

Sia disconnected the call in frustration.

His parents were out of town for the weekend and he had locked himself in his room with her memories.

He played their favourite song on repeat till he could take it no longer. Then he turned to what helped him cope with the pain the best. By the end of the night, there was a collection of liquor bottles at the foot of his bed.

As he scrolled through her profile on Facebook, he came across a post that suddenly made sense to him.

Never be dependent on one person because if they fail to be by your side, you will lose all your strength. You'll be buried under the weight of it all, waiting for that one person to pull you up. If they fail to show up, you'll be crushed. Learn to make your scars your strength instead.

He was so overcome with emotion that he proceeded to smash the wind chime that was tinkling half-heartedly. It was, after all, a gift from her. He often hoped that destroying the tangible memories associated with her would lessen his pain, but the harder he tried, the worse it got.

How could someone who had hurt him so much still be on his mind? Was the smile that he fell for not innocent but misleading? He felt like he was dealing with a coin with heads but no tails, chasing after probabilities and delusions. At that moment, it wasn't about his unrequited love, it was about her identity. Surely he could not make up such a beautiful face. But then who was the girl whose absence had shattered him? What had happened to her all of a sudden? Was she safe in the darkness of the city? The only person who had kept him sane these past few days was Sia.

Dear Diet, Let's Break Up

'Sia, that's not for you. Your salad is over there.'

'What difference is one bite going to make?' Sia was pissed off because of the never-ending dietary restrictions her mom had put in place.

'No means no.'

'Fine, I don't want to eat anything.' She pushed her chair back in anger and stormed into her bedroom, locking the door behind her.

Sia's mom had made *chole bhature* for her dad but she was not allowed to touch it. As usual, her food was served separately as instructed by a distant relative who was a dietician. Sia absolutely hated this so-called health food because it tasted like shit to her. Ever since she was a kid, she loved to eat no matter how she was feeling. When she was depressed, food made her feel better, and when she was happy, food made her happier.

However, everyone in her life made her feel bad about being overweight. Relatives would constantly comment and strangers would stare at her whenever she stepped out of her house. Gradually, she started believing that no one liked her and lost her confidence. She absolutely hated how her parents had restricted her diet.

Despite her mother constantly knocking on her bedroom door, she went to sleep hungry. She woke up in the middle of the night with a growling stomach. She placed her hands on her belly, her fingers forming a triangle. This, according to her, silenced the growling. But unable to take it any longer, she went to the kitchen and grabbed a bag of chips, a plate of cookies and the chole bhature. Placing all the food on her bedside table, she got into bed and put on her favourite Netflix show.

She was awake when her alarm rang. Smacking the clock out of habit, she changed into her uniform. She then rushed outside because she liked reaching school early.

Her mother's eyes roamed over her body in disgust. Sia was about to head out, her lunch box in hand, when her parents made her sit down at the dining table.

'Did you sneak into the kitchen last night?' her mom sounded stern.

'Mom, I was hungry. Do you want me to die of hunger?'

'You could have eaten the salad I made for you instead of throwing it into the trash.'

'I hate the health food you give me, Mom. I don't feel like eating it at all. Is that so difficult for you to understand?' Sia banged her fist on the table and got up to leave, which is when her dad ordered her to sit.

'What have you decided to do after school?'

'I don't understand. Where did this discussion about my career come from? I thought we were still arguing over last night's dinner.' Sia was surprised. 'My board exams are still a year away. I hope you are aware . . .' She thought about giving him a reality check but that's something that shouldn't be tried in front of an Indian parent.

'Don't try to act smart with me. I am your dad and not vice versa.'

A typical reply from a dad! As if I don't know who is who, thought Sia.

'I want to be a fashion designer.'

'Wow, a fashion designer? Every day we get to hear about your weight from colleagues, neighbours and relatives. I hope you realize that this will affect your marriage prospects. Now we have to deal with this additional fashion designing drama. Is this why we are trying so hard to get you admission to one of the best science colleges? Sorry, we are not ready for this gimmick of yours.'

'Dad, we don't live in a village where people have never heard of fashion designing. Also, I never asked you to get me admission to a science college. You are both forcing me, along with that idiotic lady with the aptitude test who said I was good at science.'

'You won't understand right now. You are still a kid.'

A standard reply from parents when they don't have answers to your questions, thought Sia with irritation.

'No, Dad. I am not. And how are weight and marriage related? Should marriage be my only goal in life? If that's the case, how does it matter if I choose science, commerce or arts?'

'Of course they are related. If you stay overweight, no one will marry you,' her mom said. 'We are a simple family. Things like fashion designing are not for us. Look at how focused your friend Amyra is. She has already decided to take science after school. At least take some inspiration from her.'

It's annoying when you are criticized for your decisions early in the morning. However, what's even more annoying is when your friend is praised for hers and only you know the truth. All you can really do is nod and agree.

'Can I just live my life normally, Mom?' Sia knew she would never win an argument with her parents.

'Of course you can. But being fat is not normal.'

Sia stormed out without saying a word.

She knew she wanted to be a fashion designer but she had almost been convinced to take science by her parents. She could still pursue a fashion designing course after higher secondary school. After all, she just needed some time to make them understand. They had a lot of misconceptions about the world of fashion because of the movies that they had seen. It was her passion and she wanted to show the world that she could be successful at it. All she wanted from her parents was their support. Even if they weren't satisfied with her appearance, she wanted them to support her choice of career.

Her weight was another problem. Because of her parents and the kids at school, she had lost the confidence to interact with people which was essential if she wanted to be a fashion designer. She hated it when people called her fat; she would cover up by laughing along. She hated that she couldn't wear certain types of clothes despite her love for designing them. She also hated how she was required to suck in her stomach while taking pictures.

Most of all, she hated to think that she would never have a love life because boys weren't interested in girls her size. She was fifteen and most of her friends had already kissed or were in relationships. No boy would look past all the skinny girls. She thought it was unfair how men with beer bellies were never criticized for their appearance, but as soon as a girl was slightly chubby, it was the end of the world. The only person in school who never commented on her weight was Amyra. Although she wasn't very close to her, she liked her a lot. There was just one minor issue. Amyra was insanely beautiful and Sia had a crush on Ishaan, who happened to be Amyra's boyfriend.

'Amyra! Wake up, you lazy girl!'

Amyra groaned at her younger sister's voice. She opened her eyes and looked at her watch.

'Nivi, I still have over an hour till school starts. You should go study.' She waved her arms around, hitting Nivi on the face.

'You don't want to be late on the first day of the week, do you?' Amyra's mom yelled.

Full of life, Amyra believed in spreading happiness and positivity. Many of the girls at school envied her because the boys would drool over her. The boys would stay away from her on Raksha Bandhan and run after her on Friendship Day. She never cared about what people thought of her clothes and the way she carried herself. She loved to flaunt her looks like most teenage girls and didn't mind a few stares. She enjoyed making people feel comfortable in their own skin. It was her inner beauty and kindness that made her even more desirable. By making people feel happy with what they had, she made them feel important. Being in her company was like being warmed by the sun's rays, regardless of the weather.

Amyra was not a morning person at all and getting up for school was no less than a *Roadies* task for her.

As her mom yelled, she realized that she had planned to meet Ishaan and Pihu before school. After getting dressed in a hurry, she reached school only to find that Ishaan was yet to arrive. For the next half an hour, she wandered around—the only person on campus apart from her was the schoolkeeper. She would have passed the time on her phone if only she was allowed to carry it with her. She hated school rules for this particular reason. However, she hated Ishaan and Pihu more than the rule book because they never followed any.

'Hi, baby,' Ishaan greeted her after he finally arrived.

'Hey, Ishaan. You are so early today,' she said sarcastically, feeling proud of herself for getting there first.

'Amyra, I am so sorry,' he began but Amyra cut him off.

'Ishaan, we decided to come early and study for the upcoming exams. It's the first day and you are half an hour late. I have been walking around aimlessly waiting for you. Even Pihu is not here and her mom said she had left for school. I don't know where she has disappeared. Everyone must think I am a lunatic loner. How could you do this to me?' She raised one eyebrow and waited for an excuse which was probably going to be stupid.

'I am really sorry. I slept late yesterday and completely forgot we were supposed to meet early. I jumped out of bed as soon as I remembered our plan. I promise I'll make it up to you.' He gave her a puppy-dog look.

As she stared at him, she didn't see the Ishaan that every girl fell for. The Ishaan every girl fell for was always well dressed in an ironed uniform, polished shoes and nicely done hair that complemented his smile. The Ishaan in front of her was very different. His unkempt hair fell over his eyebrows, and his red-rimmed eyes and scruffy uniform showed that he had hardly slept. Amyra couldn't help but smile at the naughty thought that popped into her head.

'You're forgiven,' she assured him with a hug.

There seemed to be no one else on campus and Ishaan pulled her close to kiss her.

'Lovebirds, I am sorry to interrupt you.' Pihu had finally reached school.

Before Amyra exploded in anger, Pihu began mimicking her.

'Where the hell were you? How can you be so careless? You just don't care about promises. I woke up early to meet you, blah, blah, blah.'

'Shut up, you asshole,' screamed Amyra.

'Okay sorry.'

'I don't want to hear any lame excuses.' Amyra started walking towards the washroom. Pihu joined her.

'I can join you inside, no one will know. It'll be a thrilling first time,' Ishaan said teasingly.

'Stay away,' Amyra said as he stepped inside.

Once inside, Pihu and Amyra began their regular gossip session.

'I plan to play football with DJ. He asked me out yesterday,' Pihu revealed while combing her hair.

'Football?' asked Amyra, looking confused.

'I mean I plan to lose my virginity.' Pihu's tone implied that this was obvious. 'Have you lost yours?' Amyra looked uncomfortable. 'What's so strange about it? You should also proceed with Ishaan.'

'He did mention it indirectly, but we're still not physical with each other.'

'Don't tell me you haven't even kissed him yet.'

'Leave me alone, you bitch!'

Amyra and Pihu were sisters from another mister and they stood by each other through both the good and bad times. Every time Amyra was annoyed because of her studies, she would go to Pihu for reassurance. Once, while swimming, her left leg had a cramp and she lost consciousness. She woke up by the poolside to see Pihu looking at her with tears in her eyes. She had jumped in the pool to pull her out!

As usual, Sia reached school early because she felt peaceful when no one was around. She felt safe as this was the only time she didn't have to worry about the stares and the laughter that followed her wherever she went. She was taken by surprise when she saw Ishaan leaning against the girls' washroom door. Every time she saw him, her heart skipped a beat. Despite knowing that she could never express her attraction to him, she couldn't help falling for him. Everyone has a secret, and this happened to be hers.

'Sia, what are you doing here at this hour?' Ishaan called out to her, bringing her back to reality.

She let out a deep sigh, realizing that she had been holding her breath.

Get a grip, Sia, she screamed internally. *Why am I so nervous? I mean, it's just Ishaan. Yeah, it's Ishaan and you like him.* She ignored the internal monologue and tried to play cool.

'Uh, you look cute in this messy attire.' *I seriously need to pull myself together.*

'Thank you so much, Sia.' He smiled, oblivious to how it got her heart racing.

He needs to stop smiling at me like that or I'll end up doing something stupid.

'What are you doing in front of the girls' washroom?'

'I am waiting for Amyra.'

'Oh.'

'Actually Amyra and I thought we'd discuss some topics for the upcoming exams.'

At that moment, Amyra and Pihu returned and their eyes landed on Sia.

'Morning, Sia,' they said in unison.

'Hey, I'll see you guys in class,' she said before walking away.

Although she was friends with them, she didn't want to get in their way. She didn't want to disturb them, but she sat in the corridor expecting Amyra to ask her to join them. However, nothing of that sort happened, which made her feel worthless and lonely.

A group of girls who mocked her every day came by instead.

'Why are you still here? We asked you to change schools, didn't we?'

'Yes, you did. Now get the fuck out of my way. I want to go to the class.'

She tried to push the girls and walk away.

'Not so fast, sweetheart. I wonder where you got your skirt stitched, considering your size.' The girls burst out laughing.

Sia was tired of hearing the same thing every single day. *Don't they have anything else to do?*

Attempting to hide her thighs, she pulled her skirt down and lowered her backpack. She pushed the girls aggressively and they didn't resist. As she entered the class, the students stared at her like they did every day. They pointed to her skirt that exposed her thighs, her fat legs, her prominent tummy and her double chin.

'Are you okay?' Amyra asked as she sat on the bench in front.

Sia gave Amyra a blank stare. She wasn't used to people being kind and didn't know how to react. It was like someone had said they loved her. These were just three random words to Amyra, which was visible from the simple manner in which she had said them but to Sia they meant the whole world.

'Yes, but why bother asking when you ignored me in the morning?'

'Why do you bother answering?' Amyra replied.

'Sorry.'

Amyra smiled to assure her that it was all right. The class ended but the teacher asked Sia to stay behind.

The bell rang and everyone, except Sia, left for the sports period. Her teacher walked towards her while going through her handbag. She finally took out what she was looking for and sat in front of Sia.

'Is there something wrong?' Sia asked.

'Well, darling, you see, I noticed how you look when you're in class. I thought this might make you feel better.'

She placed two small bottles on her desk. Sia looked at her in confusion when she read the label: *For burning fat and speeding up the process of losing weight. This will turn you from fat and thick to skinny and slim.*

'Use it well because it is expensive. I got this for you to make you feel better.'

'Did my parents put you up to this?'

'No, darling. You are a bright student and I don't want such things to affect your grades.'

Picking up the bottles, Sia walked out of the classroom in a hurry.

'I'm sorry and thank you,' she shouted after her.

She ran down the stairs to the back of the building where she knew no one would disturb her. As the tears streamed down her cheeks, she thought about how badly she wanted to cut away the extra fat on her body with a pair of scissors. If only it were that simple.

The innocence on her face was disappearing day by day. The constant worry about her appearance had taken a toll on her mental health, which showed on her face. She was constantly fearful of hanging out with people and barely had any close friends. As she obsessively read magazines that contained tips about how to lose weight in a matter of days, sometimes even instantly, she began hating her body and herself even more.

Her life in school became almost unbearable once Amyra suddenly left the school before the beginning of their final year. The pressure of the board exams and the constant commentary on her body added to her sense of hopelessness. Ishaan was the only support she had after Amyra shifted to another school for reasons unknown to Sia. She tried asking Ishaan what had happened, but he avoided giving her an answer. Even Pihu had taken a year off. She didn't know what had happened among the three friends, but she knew something was terribly wrong.

However, this didn't mean that she began interacting with Ishaan more regularly. On the contrary, she even stopped talking to him to limit her distractions before the exams. She knew her parents would give her hell if she scored below their expectations. Amidst all the stress, her desire to become a fashion designer was slowly fading.

Level College Unlocked

It is said that time is the solution to all problems but, with time, Sia only found her life becoming more complicated. After scoring excellent marks in her board exams, she landed up in a science college, crushing her dreams to live the life her parents wanted for her. With time, mobile screens became larger but her parents remained small-minded. She didn't stay in touch with any of her school friends because she wanted to start afresh. It wasn't like anyone from her class had tried to keep in touch with her either. Even her absence from the school farewell party went unnoticed.

Amyra had changed schools before the boards and completely disappeared from Sia's life. This was until Sia sent her a friend request on Facebook. The first person to come to her mind on opening an account on

Facebook during the summer vacation was Amyra. She had only seventy-five friends on Facebook, of which fifty were random requests that she had accepted and some were relatives. She never expressed herself on her account and restricted herself to just reading her newsfeed.

Her profile picture was of a cute cartoon that she had found online. She didn't show her face. She only uploaded a few photographs clicked from angles meant to make her look thinner. These photographs were only uploaded on Amyra's insistence.

She thought Sia's profile, with no real photographs, was a fake account when she received a friend request. It was clear that being overweight still tormented Sia. She still believed that no one loved her. The bullying had become worse in college as there were no strict rules imposed on the students. Names like 'fatso', 'fatty' and 'hippo' followed her everywhere. Deciding what to wear to college every day was torture.

That day was no different. After rejecting almost every outfit in her closet—some made her thighs look big, while others made her breasts look uneven—she decided on a pair of culottes. Before she left home, she checked Facebook messenger to see an unread message from Amyra which made her feel better.

Finally got admission after the last round and guess what? I'm coming to your college!

After leaving school in ninth grade, Amyra had shifted to one closer to her new house in Versova. She still felt guilty about leaving and losing touch with Ishaan and Pihu, who were certainly hurt. But with the pressure of adapting to a new place and the board exams, she lost track of her old friends. This affected her grades which is why she had to wait till the final round to get admission to a college. Sia was the one person she knew there since all her friends from school had opted for the commerce stream. This is why she had messaged Sia on Facebook a day before joining.

After chatting online for a while, they exchanged numbers and decided to meet. Although Sia was very happy about Amyra coming to the same college as her, meeting her for the first time in two years scared her. She thought she wouldn't know what to say and kept practising questions intended to break the ice. She cursed herself for not being outgoing enough.

Will she be the same Amyra I knew? Will she really be friends with me in college? Yes, I have lost some weight since school but will she be judgemental? No, she wasn't during our schooldays. But it was not like she was my best friend. Plus, she dated my crush.

The lectures had already begun, but Sia waited for Amyra. Sitting in the canteen alone, she was about to text her when she heard a familiar voice behind her.

'Hey! How are you?' asked Sia.

'I am fine, what about you? I am happy to see you after so long.' Amyra took a seat opposite her.

'Yes, it's been a while. How did you recognize me?'

'You have not changed a bit. It wasn't difficult to spot you.'

Sia eased a bit and hearing Amyra's words made her feel happy.

'I see you don't come to college early like you did in school.'

Amyra laughed, remembering the good old days.

'Even you used to come early.'

'Not always. But why did you leave the school so suddenly? I searched your Facebook friends list for Pihu but couldn't find her. The two of you were like sisters. Also I heard Ishaan and you—'

'We are not in touch because of personal reasons.'

Hearing Amyra's tone, Sia realized that she didn't want to talk about her sudden change of schools. But Sia sensed that there was more to the matter than she was letting on. Amyra's expression had changed completely to one of sadness on hearing Pihu's name. Sia let the matter rest as she thought it wasn't the right time.

Amyra had made sure that the incident that forced her to part ways with Pihu was known only to a few people from school, including Ishaan. What happened was unintentional, but its impact led to the three best friends turning away from each other forever.

'I broke up with Ishaan, your crush,' Amyra finally said with a mischievous grin.

'Fuck! You knew?'

'The entire school knew. We could all see it in the way you stared at him all the time.' Amyra couldn't stop laughing.

'I never wanted to sleep with him. It was just an infatuation.'

'Don't lie to me. You used to fuck him every day with your eyes.'

'Maybe I did. But in my defence, he was gorgeous! You were so lucky.'

'No, I wasn't. He was a pathetic kisser which turned me off.'

'You never had . . .'

'No. We didn't even kiss after the time he almost chewed off my lips.'

'What?'

'Yes, my lower lip swelled up. Anyone would have guessed that I had been kissing someone. Pihu and I tried to hide it by applying lipstick, cream and whatnot, but nothing worked. My parents would have killed me if I went home looking like that. Finally, we went to a paan shop to apply some ice and the vendor realized what we were trying to do. He came up with an idea that worked.'

'What was it?'

'He told me to tell my parents that I smacked my face against a pole on the bus which made my lower lip swell. Surprisingly, it worked!'

This had Sia ROFLing! After talking for a little while longer, they went to the administrative office to complete the formalities necessary for Amyra's enrolment. Instead of attending lectures that day, Sia helped Amyra with all her paperwork.

Where are you? Sia texted Amyra the moment she entered the chemistry lab and found her missing.

It was their first chemistry practical session and Sia wanted Amyra to come before partners were allotted. The lab sessions for each subject were to start this week as the admissions process was finally over. The people they paired themselves with would remain their lab partners for the entire duration of the course and Sia wanted Amyra to be hers. Not wanting to be paired with a complete stranger, she frantically tried calling Amyra when she didn't respond to her WhatsApp message. The class stood around random tables, waiting for the professor to enter. When he did, he asked everyone to pair up with a friend after taking attendance.

Sia acted like she was texting to avoid interacting with anyone. After most people had selected their partners, the few remaining ones, including Sia, looked at each other awkwardly.

'Why are you standing idle? Go to table four,' the professor instructed Sia.

Table four was occupied by a boy and girl who looked like they were a couple. Completely engrossed in each other, they ignored Sia's weak attempt at a greeting. After the briefing, when everyone started performing the experiment, Sia simply stood at the table as if she were invisible.

'Hi, I am Sia.'

'So? Please don't interfere in our business,' the girl replied, with a look of annoyance. Embarrassed, Sia turned her gaze towards the rest of the room, hoping for Amyra to enter. The guy on the next table noticed her discomfort. He also noticed the sadness in her eyes. Intrigued, he tried starting a conversation.

'Hi.'

Taken aback, Sia stared at him for a few seconds, thinking he might have made a mistake. No stranger had ever tried to befriend her, especially not one who looked like that.

'I am Ritvik.'

She didn't know how to react when she realized that it wasn't a mistake and he really was trying to start a conversation with her. In sixteen years, this was the first time someone had actually taken the first step. She continued to stare at him in shock.

'At least tell me your name.' He didn't seem to be affected by her shocked expression.

'I'm Sia.'

'My friend Apurv hasn't come today. You can join me if those guys are not interested in doing it with you.'

'Doing what?'

'The chemistry practical! What did you think?'

'Get your mind out of the gutter!'

'Friends?' he asked, grinning sheepishly. He held out his hand. Looking at his face properly, she realized he was extremely good-looking. His face was very childlike, almost angelic.

Sia moved to his table but didn't shake his hand.

'Let's just stick to being partners.'

'Why are you so . . .'

'Creepy?' she completed his sentence.

'Not really.'

She felt as if the entire class was staring at them. Feeling conscious, she asked him to concentrate on the practical.

'Why are you embarrassed? Is it because you're soft, cute and a bit chubby?'

Is he for real? Why is he showing so much interest in me? Sia thought. Before she could react, her phone beeped, indicating a text from Amyra.

Can I come in? I am outside the lab. I totally forgot that we had a practical today. Only realized when I saw your text.
Come in. We've just started.

After a little hesitation, Amyra knocked on the door. To say that she looked exquisite would be an understatement. In her denim shorts and T-shirt she could have been on the cover of a magazine. But she was certainly better than those two-dimensional photoshopped models. The hesitation in her body and the softness in her voice made her even more attractive. Almost every guy in the class looked at her with desire. The professor, however, looked at his watch and gave her a stern look.

'Is this the time to come to class?'

'I am sorry, Sir. I forgot that the practical was scheduled for today. It's my first day.'

'Aren't you ashamed of coming late to class on your first day? What kind of clothes are you wearing? You should have taken admission in a commerce college if you wanted to reveal your skin rather than your brain.'

'Sorry,' Amyra responded, looking humiliated.

'What do you mean "sorry"? Your parents should at least teach you to be decent. What do you wish to prove by coming to college like this? Girls like you are real troublemakers. Next time, don't enter my lab if you're wearing such clothes. It's a lab, not a ramp.'

Amyra was embarrassed at being publicly humiliated. She could feel all the boys ogling her like she was a piece of meat. The staring never really bothered her, but today it made her feel self-conscious and angry. She left without looking at anyone and then texted Sia.

> I wish this professor has bad sex for the rest of his life.
> Do you want me to convey your message?
> Why don't you kick his balls so hard that he suffers from erectile dysfunction for a lifetime.
> LOL! Chill. I'll meet you during lunch.

With this, Sia quickly put her phone away.

Is it so difficult to accept a girl for the way she is? Why should you demean them in front of everyone and judge them for their looks and behaviour? Girls who wear tank tops and short skirts, get drunk and kiss on the first date, wear make-up and go out at night are sluts. But those who wear long-sleeved shirts and knee-length skirts, have their faces scrubbed clean and never go out are prudes.

Amyra didn't really care about the slut-shaming, having faced it so often. But it was her first day and she had been excited to go to class. She wished she could do something about it rather than ignoring it and sipping a cold drink in the canteen. She really wanted someone to tell her that there was nothing wrong with wearing what she wanted. She hoped someone would tell her that it was absolutely fine to be herself.

Leave Me Alone

'Apurv, where are you? The chemistry practical is about to start,' Ritvik said.

'I am on my way. I've just reached Dadar station.' Apurv hung up as it was impossible to get off a jam-packed train while speaking on the phone.

As he walked towards the western side, he saw a shopkeeper hitting a little beggar girl. Apurv ran towards the scene and put himself between the man and the girl.

'What's wrong?' he could barely control his anger.

'She is a thief. She took the bun and didn't pay for it.'

Apurv took out a fifty-rupee note from his pocket and handed it to the man.

'Hope this solves your problem.'

Apurv bent down and asked the little girl if she was hungry.

After a few moments of hesitation, she nodded. Her eyes were swollen, and her face looked pale. He took the rolls from his lunch box and gave them to her. Looking at the time, he ran towards the exit.

Meanwhile, Ritvik kept calling him continuously.

'I'm coming!'

'The practical has started and the professor is not allowing anyone inside now.'

'I didn't want to attend it anyway. See you during lunch.'

Apurv was not someone you would consider attractive at the first glance. But once you got to know him, you couldn't stay away. Although his coffee-coloured skin made him look handsome, he thought it was a curse. He spent hours in salons and most of his pocket money on skin-lightening products.

The tragedy of his life, according to him, was that he had never had a girlfriend. Every time he thought he was making progress with a girl, he got friend-zoned. Lately, he had started writing a blog. But this was mainly because he thought girls were mostly attracted to men with a creative bent of mind, like writers.

He went straight to the college canteen because the lunch break had almost begun.

'A Coke and a chicken sandwich please,' he ordered and stood beside the counter.

It was rush hour and everyone wanted the canteen boy to deliver their order first. Apurv was scrolling down his newsfeed on Facebook when from the corner of his eye he saw a gorgeous girl in shorts standing next to him. He didn't look up immediately as that would have made him seem like a pervert. However, he was sure that the girl was ravishing. This was his first encounter with Amyra.

The canteen boy placed a plastic cup in front of him, and he picked it up and took a big sip without looking away from his phone. He only realized it was not his order when it burnt his tongue.

'Excuse me, that's mine,' said Amyra, irritated.

Apurv finally looked towards her to apologize, but he was stunned by her beauty. He instantly developed a crush on her.

'Should I buy you another coffee? Or you can have my Coke if you want,' Apurv said after a few moments of silence.

Fuck, fuck! How could I be so silly? Mistaking coffee for Coke?

'No, thanks,' Amyra replied in a tone that suggested he had done it intentionally. She turned and walked away.

Apurv, however, stood still, his eyes following her every move.

Why does stuff like this happen to me every time? Especially when it's a girl. That too one who is super hot. I should have introduced myself at least.

While Apurv had fallen head over heels for Amyra, she was boiling with anger as she walked through the corridor. *First it was the professor and then the guy in the canteen.*

'Why are you so pissed off? Still angry about what the professor said?' Sia asked as she saw Amyra in the corridor.

'Chuck it! It's nothing. I just met an idiot in the canteen.'

'Are you okay?'

'Yes, babe. I'm just having a bad day. I should go home.'

Although Amyra dismissed Apurv as a weirdo, he couldn't think about anything but her. It got him thinking that maybe this was more than just a silly crush. Thinking about her made him smile for no reason and he felt extra motivated to go to college the next day. He felt like an idiot for not talking to her when he had the chance. He wished he could meet her again.

An entire week of college had passed but nobody opened their books. The funny thing about college was that the professors put you to sleep during their lectures in the day, while your friends kept you up at night.

Apurv and Ritvik had become close friends, but Sia kept Amyra at a distance. They only talked during their classes together. When Amyra started becoming close to their other classmates, Sia took a step back. She was wary of being in a group because she tended to become the butt of every joke. Amyra often tried to include Sia in their discussions, but she remained unsure. Soon, Amyra stopped trying.

Gradually, they limited their interactions to simple hellos and goodbyes. Apurv and Amyra crossed each other multiple times but never interacted. Amyra got over the canteen incident but Apurv didn't have the courage to start a conversation.

It was that time of the week again when Ritvik and Sia had to pair up for the chemistry practical class. Amyra decided to skip once again because of what had happened the previous week and requested Sia to mark her attendance by proxy. Apurv and Ritvik were already in the lab although there was still time for class to start.

'Are you participating in the play for the inter-college festival next semester?' Ritvik asked, playing with a piece of chalk.

'Are they allowing freshers to register too?'

'Yes. I've registered to be a voice-over artist. You should sign up for something. It'll be fun,' Ritvik suggested while sketching on the board.

'I might apply. But what are you trying to draw on the board?'

Ritvik didn't react and continued to draw the outline of what looked like a girl's face for the next few minutes. Apurv stared at the board in confusion, trying to guess who she was.

'Who is it? Looks like some fat cartoon character. Is she your girlfriend?'

'No! She's my lab partner.' Ritvik turned towards Apurv once he was done.

He wrote 'Chubby Cute Sia' beside the sketch.

'Oh, I know who she is. What's the purpose behind this? Have you been fantasizing about her?' Apurv winked.

'It's not like that, dude. This is just for fun. She thinks she is ugly but she is actually kind of cute. She feels terrible about herself.'

'Wow, bro. You've noticed a lot in just one session. Something is up for sure.'

'Stop it, dude. I just want her to look at this cute sketch of herself and feel better.'

'Really? I hope she doesn't feel the opposite. Your drawing is terrible.'

'But my intentions aren't. And that's what matters.' Ritvik smiled.

On the first day itself, Ritvik could see how much Sia hated herself. This was just an innocent attempt at making her smile without any ill intentions. He did not love her, nor was he dying to be her friend. He just sympathized with what she was going through.

'There is still half an hour before the class starts. Let's go to the registration counter and I will sign up for the play,' Apurv suggested, looking at his watch.

They walked downstairs to the registration desk. The play was meant to help students explore their creativity. Although the play was supposed to be staged next semester, the registration process had begun to filter out those who weren't good enough over the next fifty days. Apurv was signing up in the hope of meeting a girl.

On their way back to class, he spotted Amyra walking towards the main gate and immediately decided to follow her.

'Dude,' he called out to Ritvik, 'you attend chemistry while I try to improve my chemistry. Bye!'

Before Ritvik could protest, Apurv ran towards the parking lot to get his Vespa. Ritvik sighed and walked back to the lab. The sketch he had made had totally slipped his mind and he only remembered once he was a few feet away. He guessed that the professor hadn't arrived yet when he heard loud noises from inside the lab. He was relieved to a certain degree because he wanted to erase the drawing once Sia had seen it. However, the moment he entered the lab, he immediately regretted his decision. A few students were giggling while writing on the board. Ritvik was absolutely disgusted with what he saw.

His sketch was still on the board, but his classmates had added several disrespectful comments to it. They had written about Sia's bra size, that she had a baby bump without being pregnant and that she would break the bones of any guy she tried to ride during sex.

Ritvik felt guilty for being the one to provoke this bullying. If he hadn't drawn a picture of her on the board, this wouldn't have happened.

Before the professor entered, he slapped the guy who was writing these comments and rubbed the board clean. When he heard that Sia had already seen it all, he was heartbroken. He felt sorry for Sia and was sure that this incident would be a major blow to her self-esteem. He wished he had her number so he could apologize. He was too ashamed to find out if she knew that it was his drawing that had caused this.

He felt horrible thinking about how she must have felt when she looked at what they had done to his innocent sketch.

Sia was slowly accepting the way things were. She knew she couldn't focus only on her dream of being a fashion designer. She had to make sure she got good grades to keep her parents happy. Nevertheless, she kept sketching and writing down every idea she had between lectures. Most designers made clothes only for skinny girls. She wanted to design clothes for overweight people instead. She couldn't make these sketches at home because her parents were always paying close attention to what she did, making sure she studied. After all, she was a science student.

It was one of those days when she just wanted to sit at home and sketch. But since her dad was home, she decided college would be a better option. As soon as she entered the class, she knew something was wrong. They were all laughing at her, but today their laughter was different. It sounded more evil and degrading. The commotion near the board finally caught her attention. She gasped in horror when she saw how they had degraded her. They had spared nothing. There were vulgar comments about her body, her clothes and her character. Unable to take it any longer, she ran home without looking back. She didn't know who was responsible for this, but it wasn't like it mattered. They were all against her and knowing who was responsible wouldn't make her feel any better.

So much hatred just because I am overweight? she thought as she hurried home.

Instead of being concerned, her parents bombarded her with questions as soon as she walked in.

'How come you are back so early today?'

Without giving her time to respond, her dad asked, 'Why aren't you attending lectures today? You had a chemistry practical, right?'

'You won't get anywhere in life if you bunk college like this,' added her mother.

'Please leave me alone.'

She locked herself in her room because she had no strength for her parents' questions. *They can clearly see that I've had a hard day. Yet, they expect me to answer their stupid questions. Of course I'm not all right. At least my mother should be able to sense that. But all she cares about are my studies. What about my emotional needs? And Dad has become so obsessed with my career that he has forgotten about my mental well-being.* Sia buried her head in the pillows.

She felt as if she was screaming but no one could hear her. She finally felt broken beyond repair. On some days, she faked being ill and stayed at home. On others, instead of going to college, she simply wandered around. Gradually, this became her daily routine so her parents wouldn't suspect anything. Despite multiple messages from Amyra, she didn't consider going back even once. She had lost her self-confidence bit by bit and now she had finally reached her breaking point. She even took an appointment to meet the counsellor on campus but didn't go because she felt hopeless.

Like every other teenager, she was desperately seeking some sort of validation. She just wanted someone to tell her that she was worth it. She tried to make herself feel better by sketching more often but it didn't work. Out of desperation, she tried browsing the Internet for tips that would make her feel less terrible. Little did she know that this was the beginning of her path to self-destruction. She landed on a forum where people seemed to be talking about their problems, when suddenly a message flashed across the screen.

Self-harm will numb your emotional turmoil. Hurting yourself will relieve you of your inner conflict. It will give you a sense of purpose while defying socially accepted norms you are being forced to follow. Are you ready to take the challenge? If yes, click here to join the group.

Before really thinking about what she was doing, Sia joined the group. After a couple of minutes, she got a message from someone called the Curator.

Are you sure you want to take the Blue Whale Challenge?
Yes, I'm absolutely sure.
You will find what you seek. You will achieve happiness. But are you sure? There's no turning back.

Sia grew a little anxious, but she was adamant that no one could stop her.

Yes. But what do you mean there's no turning back?
You can't leave the game unfinished once you click start.

I am not a quitter. I'm ready.
Carry out each task diligently but make sure no one knows what you're doing. Send me a picture at the end of every task. At the end of the game, you die.
Die?
Yes. You will find solace. You will conquer your fears. Hurting yourself is the only way to numb your emotional disturbance.
What if I want to get out?
I have all your information, they will come after you.

Sometimes, you take drastic steps to forget about the emotional trouble you are in. Sia had been hurt so badly that she felt like nothing could hurt her any more. She looked around her room and realized that she was completely and utterly alone, in every sense. She had joined the group without giving a thought to the consequences. The fact was that as soon as she had clicked 'YES', all her data had been hacked. If she failed to perform the tasks, 'they' would come after her. All the personal information on her laptop and synced devices would be used against her.

She had to perform fifty tasks in fifty days. There was truly no turning back.

I feel chained being forced to do things I don't want to do. I am sure they are spying on me. I've tried to get out, but they won't let me, no matter how hard I try. I watched horror movies on my own and remained confined to my room and completed almost all the tasks as part of the Blue Whale Challenge. I tried escaping once, but I was blackmailed. They have all my information, from my chats to my browsing history from the day I created my Google account. I am writing this out of desperation because they are threatening to kill my parents. Someone please help me.

Sia was about to post the status when she received a message from the Curator.

If you cheat, we'll tell your parents you watched porn a few months ago.

Through remote access to her mobile, the Curator tracked everything she did on her phone. It was when she had been forced to download the Blue Whale mobile app on the fourteenth day, that she knew something was wrong. Before that, the tasks were easy and fun. The last thirty-six days had been so excruciating that she almost gave in to the strangers who were harassing her.

I didn't watch porn. That was a virus.
If that doesn't scare you, we will kill your
parents. We know their whereabouts. You and
your parents are being watched every second of
the day. You can't escape death.

Now she knew she couldn't post a status and ask for help. The words, 'You can't escape death' rang in her head. She repeated them till she felt like she was going to explode. She hated herself even more now. She was ugly, fat and now an idiot for getting caught up in something like this.

Do it now! Otherwise you'll be a failure. A fat, ugly and idiotic failure, the voices in her head screamed.

She couldn't ignore them any more. She went out of her room and looked at her parents for a moment, trying to recall her childhood. She walked out of the house and shut the door behind her with a sense of finality. It was forty-five minutes past seven.

What are you waiting for? Do it now. She suddenly felt powerful because, for once, she was taking a stand.

This is how it's supposed to feel. This is how you know you are doing it right. She was lost. She was about to win the Blue Whale Challenge at the cost of losing the challenge of life. *You can't escape death. It's the solution to all your problems, your final task in the Blue Whale Challenge.*

In a small part of her brain, she still wanted to go back to her life and friends. But she pushed that thought out of her mind when she looked around her. She had reached the college terrace, prepared to take her own life. The tears that flowed down her cheeks carried an ocean whose depths remain unexplored. As soon as the clock struck nine, Sia let the suicide note fall from her hands and stepped up on to the edge, ready to jump.

Friends, Maybe?

For the last fifty days, Apurv had been trying to talk to Amyra. He had been following her but she never really noticed him. He hadn't been entirely unsuccessful; he now knew where she lived and when she went for her evening walk.

He was scrutinizing his love life at the snack shop near the college gate.

'Do you think I'll ever be able to speak to her?'

'Yes, if you stop being a coward and actually go talk to her,' replied Ritvik. 'Just do it.'

'You think this is a Nike advert? Just do it.'

'Show some balls.'

'I think we should leave. It's already nine.' Apurv picked up his backpack.

They were usually home by this time but that night they had been engrossed in playing Counter-Strike at the cybercafe near college. When Apurv stepped out of the snack shop, he saw a figure on the terrace, standing dangerously close to the edge. He realized in horror that it was a person.

'Fuck! That student is trying to jump off!' He ran to the building through the main gate with Ritvik close on his heels.

'Don't you think we should call the guard?'

'There's no time and that idiot doesn't seem to be around. He must be on his phone somewhere.' Apurv sped up as he climbed the stairs.

When he finally reached the terrace, he saw a girl standing on the edge. He had never been in such a delicate situation before. He knew that if he made even one wrong move, a life would be lost. He had only seen things like this in movies. He was very scared.

Ritvik's eyes widened in horror when he realized who the girl was.

'Sia, I am sorry. I am really sorry.'

Apurv looked at Ritvik in confusion.

'Sia, please forgive me.' Ritvik's voice rose to a scream when Sia didn't respond.

Sia knew that if she turned back, the Curator would do something bad. But she wanted to speak to Ritvik once before taking her life.

What difference is speaking to him going to make? She knew she had to jump to save her family.

However, Ritvik's apologies finally made her step down from the edge.

'Why are you sorry?'

'I didn't mean to do that,' said Ritvik, assuming that it was the lab incident that had pushed her to the edge. Little did he know that she was not even aware of it.

'Didn't mean to do what?'

'What's happening?' Apurv interrupted.

They said nothing.

Apurv picked up the note that was on the ground. Sia tried snatching it from him but he refused to let go.

'Stop meddling in my life!' she screamed at him. But he gave her a stern look and began reading.

My name is Sia and I am a sixteen-year-old girl from Mumbai. By the time you read this, I will be gone. I want to warn everyone against playing the Blue Whale Challenge because if those people could do this to me, they could do it to anyone. I was mentally tortured and threatened by the Curator. They took advantage of my depression. It was not just the Curator. Everyone taunted me for being fat, for not looking perfect. I tried to be strong but I am tired. I just can't handle it any more.

Apurv tore the piece of paper to shreds and looked at Sia. She was visibly shaken. She was shivering so much that she could hardly stand. Apurv took her by the shoulders and helped her sit on the water tank.

'Please leave me alone. They will kill you too.'

Apurv just stared at her. He understood what she was going through. Her heart had so much emotion and she had caged it all. He could see it in her eyes. He was quite sure that the step she had taken was no less than a criminal offence but he just wanted to make her feel better, make her feel like life was worth living.

'Calm down. No one is watching us.'

She scanned the terrace in fear. Realizing that there really was no one nearby, she relaxed a little. However, her body continued to shake. Apurv took her phone and, after deleting all the apps and her Gmail account, smashed it with an iron rod that he found on the terrace.

'What the fuck are you doing?' Sia screamed in surprise.

'Chill. Your fear is hiding inside this phone. Simply throw it away. Buy a new SIM card and phone and open a new Gmail account. They won't be able to trace your new number or account. I read it recently in the newspaper. So relax.'

'Will this work?'

'Trust me, it will.'

'My parents will be worried,' Sia looked at her phone.

'If you really cared about your parents, you wouldn't be here. They would never have seen you again. That was your plan, right?'

Sia didn't respond. Apurv picked up her phone. 'You mean they will worry about your broken phone. Since you're still alive, your phone holds more value. If it were otherwise, your life would have taken all the credit. No one would have cared about this poor phone.'

Sia couldn't help but smile. For the first time in days she actually had a genuine grin on her face. She was not sure whether it was Apurv or how close she came to losing her life.

'Do you sympathize with the phone? Poor baby, no one cares about it. They smashed it without thinking about its feelings. Damn.'

'No, no,' laughed Sia.

'Her name is Sia,' Ritvik interrupted.

'I thought she was Carbs,' said Apurv.

'Carbs?'

'Ya. Hi, Carbs.'

'What do you mean? I am not Carbs.'

'Exactly! You are not fat, you have fat. You are not Carbs, you have carbs. You also have fingernails but you are not fingernails.'

Sia was stunned. This was the first time someone had actually made an effort to make her smile. For her, nice people existed only in the books that she read.

'Thanks. I am really thankful for your kind words. But I know you don't mean it. Don't worry, I won't jump,' Sia said with absolutely no expression on her face. But somewhere inside she was still smiling.

'No, I really mean it. I think you are beautiful. It's just that you have masked yourself. Anyone who told you otherwise was blinded by a very narrow standard of beauty. When you look at yourself, why do you think about their opinions? Why do you let them do this to you? You gave them the right to hurt you emotionally and they did. Just being skinny is not beautiful. Feeling good about yourself can also make you feel beautiful. If the world doesn't feel so, the world is blind.'

With every minute she spent with Apurv, Sia's smile widened. For the first time that she could remember, she felt good about herself. But she was scared about this ending badly.

'Why are you being so nice to me?'

'Actually, I should get paid for this motivational speech.' Apurv crossed his arms, a fake look of anger on his face.

'Shut up.'

'We should leave before someone catches us,' warned Ritvik.

'You're right. Someone might think we are having a threesome on the terrace in the moonlight.'

In the past couple of hours, life had showed Sia two sides of a coin—one reflected hatred for her body, her looks, her failures and her entire existence, and the other reflected kindness, love and acceptance for the same things, making her realize that it was all her perception. Within no time, she felt really comfortable with Apurv, like she didn't have to pretend to be nice.

'Stop hating yourself. Start loving yourself. Stop seeing yourself through their prejudiced eyes. Stop letting society's impossible expectations bring you down. All my friends expect me to be in a relationship. But I am single. I've never even kissed anyone,' said Apurv.

'You are crazy.'

'No, don't think I'm trying to flirt with you.'

'It's okay. I've got it.'

Once they were off the campus, Ritvik urged Apurv to drop Sia home on his Vespa. However, Sia was a little hesitant.

'Don't worry. You won't be my first kiss.'

'Thanks for that.' Sia agreed because even if she hardly knew him, he had saved her life and made her feel positive. She had begun to trust him already. On the way home, Apurv made her promise that she would attend college regularly. She also agreed to buy him a coffee from the college canteen. They spent the entire ride talking and Apurv gave her his number. As soon as he reached home, Apurv received a message on WhatsApp.

> *Thank you for whatever you did today. It means a lot to me.*
> *Whose number is this?*
> *My mom's. I'll buy a new phone tomorrow.*
> *Okay. But don't forget to delete the chat before you sleep or else I will be at the top of the college building tomorrow.*
> *Thank you again. But did you really mean those words?*
> *Of course.*
> *Don't think I am flirting with you. I still won't be your first kiss.*

Sia had made sure her mom was asleep before taking her phone that was on charge in the living room. In the dark, the screen flashed with Apurv's reply.

> *Ha, ha. On a serious note, I meant it. People are going to insult you, criticize you and judge you for things that you have no control over. People are going to convince you through their words and actions that you are not good enough. Fight the urge to believe them because they don't know who you are.*

*I know. But it hurts. It's easy for you to say
such things.*

*I completely understand. But the only
difference between you and them is the amount
of validation they get from society. But then
again, that isn't beauty. That is just approval.
So yes, you may be unconventional, but you are
beautiful.*

Friends?

*Damn, I thought we were already friends. Oh,
I see. For you, friendship only begins with a
friend request on Facebook.* ☺

Get lost. Bye. See you tomorrow.

Sia put her mom's phone back on charge and deleted
the chat before going to sleep. She couldn't remember
the last time she had gone to sleep without any bad
dreams or thoughts. Apurv had managed to make her
believe that her worth was not tied to a number on a
weighing scale.

When she woke up it felt like a new morning. She felt
different in a good way.

Nothing had changed. She still weighed the same
but after coming out of the shower, when she saw her
body in the mirror, she accepted it wholeheartedly. She

felt slightly nervous because she was going to college after a long time and had to face all her professors. What scared her more than that was the thought of all the students making fun of her. Apurv had promised her that he would be waiting at the gate in the morning and sure enough, there he was.

'Morning, Carbs.'

'Shut up, you freaking ass.'

'You owe me a coffee.'

'Certainly.'

The passage to the canteen was not easy for her mentally. She remembered the way she had run out of the lab and the college through the same passage. She could feel every eye in the corridor staring at her, just like on that day. Apurv sensed the discomfort in her walk and held her hand. She immediately pulled it back because she knew that he would be mocked because of her. But Apurv held it again with a strong grip and she glanced at him. Was he an angel? She wished he had come into her life earlier. With each step towards the canteen, holding his hand and ignoring the world around her, the fear on her face was replaced by a blushing smile.

'I wish we were friends in school.'

'You sound like you are the mother of two kids on the verge of retiring from life.'

'Are you always like this?'

'Like what?'

'Trying to act cool?' Sia responded with a wry smile.

After looking at each other for a moment, waiting for the other to react, they burst out laughing. 'Which coffee would you like?'

'Cappuccino.'

The canteen was mostly full of couples who had bunked the early morning lectures and a few nerds who sipped coffee with their heads buried deep into their books. As she stood in the line to order, Sia thought, *I hope this is not a dream because if it is, I will be back to square one. I don't want to lose a friend like Apurv. No one has ever given me this much importance, not even my parents. Aren't we somewhat similar? How do I feel about him? He makes me so comfortable. He makes me love myself, that's what matters. He's my first real connection.*

'Madam, your coffee.' The canteen boy brought her back to reality. With an awkward smile, she returned to the table. Apurv, who was messaging someone, kept his phone aside once she sat down opposite him.

'So you lost your self-esteem, everyone broke up with you and you're alone.' Apurv summarized after Sia told him her story. 'Big deal!'

'It isn't? Tell me about something else that happened in your life.'

He had summed up her life in two words. 'I am just saying, what's done is done. Think of the positive things. You've got a friend like me and you are actually coming out of your shell. Don't you see the difference?'

She noticed that, for the first time, she was not bothered by the stares of the people sitting around her.

'Have you even looked at yourself? It's clear how much more relaxed you are.'

'You've never had a girlfriend?'

'Don't change the topic.'

'I am serious.'

'Not even one. I always paid for my own movie tickets while my couple friends bought one-on-one. Kinda boring, right?' Apurv sipped his coffee.

'Not really. At least you didn't have to share your samosa.'

For the next few hours, their banter continued. She felt like she could go on talking for hours and still not get enough of him. She had expressed her emotions so strongly for the first time as no one ever showed an interest in knowing her in and out.

'You know, I've always wanted to be a designer,' she confessed to Apurv.

'Wow! That's cool. But then what are you doing in this fucking science college?'

'Fucking living my parents' dream.'

'Fucking dumb you are then. Anyway, you can still design after you complete your HSC. Don't give up on it.'

She knew it wasn't as easy as this but she didn't drag the topic.

'Have you always wanted to study science?'

'Yes, but I write too.'

'Okay, let me guess, you want to be an engineer, right?'

'Ya! A techie.'

'Not surprising. All the authors I read are engineers. Do you want to be like them?'

'I have no such plans as of now. But I love the attention writers get from girls.' After a brief pause, he added, 'Has anyone told you that your voice is sweet? I mean it has a lot of authority.'

'Are you trying to flatter me?'

'No, no. I'm actually trying to convince you to register for the college play.'

'Play?' she responded in shock.

'Yeah, as a female voice-over artist. It'll be fun. I have registered for scriptwriting. Otherwise college life is boring. Do you want to read my writing? I wrote this yesterday. It not only talks about your situation but also mine. A girl who's always in the plan B category.'

'Do you think you are the second choice for girls?'

'Of course. Do you want to check out the Fair & Handsome cream in my bag? It doesn't seem to be working.'

Sia grinned and Apurv handed over a sheaf of papers to her. He had written from a girl's perspective.

As someone who belongs to the plan B category,
I'm not someone who grabs your attention. I'm

not extraordinarily good-looking. But it's when I speak that I capture your attention. That, unfortunately, is not enough. No one wants to hook up with an average-looking girl no matter how good she is at holding a conversation. This is what the hook-up culture in college is about, right? But I will not be your second choice. I can stand my own and I have a heart that demands attention.

'Well done, Mr Writer,' Sia said once she had finished reading the piece.

Sia really appreciated Apurv's way of thinking and his approach to life. He never took life very seriously. For him, his friends and close ones mattered more than anything. He knew how to sweet-talk them, the way he managed to convince Sia to register for the play. He belonged to the category of guys who always waited for someone else to cut the first turf. Once that was done, he knew how to handle relationships. Sia knew that she could never be as convincing as him, but she also knew that his friendship would end up meaning a lot to her. She was slowly and gradually opening up and letting Apurv explore the depths of her personality. Like the sea, she was profound, and Apurv the sailor watched her reveal herself bit by bit.

Sip, Sip, Hooray!

Watching her from a distance is all I can do for now. She suddenly looked in my direction and even though she could not see me, I held my breath in awe. As I gazed at those beautiful eyes and her flawless face, I was ravished by the attention she unknowingly gave me. She had only looked at me for a second but it felt like a million years. She turned away, but the stalker in me wanted her to look at me again. Ever since I saw her that day in the canteen, I knew I had to follow her, learn her ways and win her heart in my own way.

Apurv wrote on his notepad as he waited on the street to be able to see her. He hoped that one day she would notice him and start a conversation, but it felt like he would have to wait forever. He had even tried working out at the same gym as her but she didn't even notice him. Everyone—from the cafe manager to the paan *tapri* guy—had noticed him on the street near her house every day, except Amyra. That day he was determined to strike up a conversation with her. He thought the same thing each day but today he was more determined than ever.

He had been waiting for more than an hour and was about to order a Coke when he saw her coming out of her gate. Even in casual clothes, she looked no less than a princess. She acted as an instant energy booster and all his tiredness faded away in a second.

It was around 2 p.m. and there were not too many people on the street. He exited the cafe and sat on his Vespa but dropped the plan of driving. Instead, he started walking in her direction while combing his hair. He nervously rubbed his hands as he inched closer. Lost in her own world with her headphones plugged in, she effortlessly walked towards him while every step took tremendous effort for Apurv. His heart skipped a beat when he saw her just a few metres away.

Fuck, she should be a therapist, she can easily hypnotize anyone. I think I should turn back, I just can't do this. No, it will look so weird if I turn suddenly in the middle of the road. Who does that? One second you are walking north and the other second you turn

58

south. I will look idiotic. I should speak. Come on, Apurv, go for it.

'Hi,' he muttered, his face expressionless.

His greeting went unnoticed because she had headphones on. By the time he realized this, she had already crossed him.

Damn, I am such an idiot, Apurv thought and turned again.

'Hi.' This time he was louder and Amyra heard him.

Apurv froze when she moved her hands to remove the headphones. He wished he could live such moments every day. He just couldn't stop himself from staring at her.

'Sorry?'

'I said, "Hi".'

She looked angry.

'I mean, is there a Starbucks somewhere around here?' Apurv was nervous and began making stuff up. 'My friend is waiting for me there and asking elderly people about a coffee shop doesn't make sense. Only you looked young enough around here to know where it might be. The data on my phone is also not working or else I would have checked Google Maps.'

'It's that way. Go straight and take a left.'

'Thank you.'

She smiled and left, but he stood there looking like an idiot.

Absolute shit. Fine. Whatever. I'll just date myself. He had completely mastered the art of doing the right things the wrong way. As he left, Apurv hoped she would attend the freshers' party that evening. The damage had already been done and he desperately needed a doctor to cure his pain, a trainer to teach him to swim, a coach to make him run, and an officer to teach him the tricks of the trade as he clearly didn't know anything.

Back home, Apurv was waiting for his dad to leave for his evening shift. He wanted to use his dad's razor to shave for the very first time. Although he hardly had any stubble, he wanted to look perfect that night.

Once his dad left, he opened his shaving kit and fished out the razor, a small tube of shaving cream and the brush. Before he started, he watched a few YouTube videos to get it right. After examining the angles perfectly, he rubbed his palm on his chin and slowly started spreading the foam from his cheekbones all the way down to his chin. He didn't need that much but it was fun. Next, he picked up the razor and placed it on his cheek. His hand trembled but with one stroke he moved the blade down to his chin. Dipping the razor in a mug of water, he repeated the process.

'Ouch!' he screamed in pain. Overconfidence kills your happiness, they say. It had made a gash on Apurv's face.

It looked so easy in the video. Now my freshers' night is ruined. He had no courage to finish shaving.

Shit happens! I mean look at your face, he said to himself looking into the mirror. He was confused about whether or not to attend the party. He finally gave in when both Ritvik and Sia forced him to join them. The plan had been to pick Sia up first and then get going, but she was already on her way while Ritvik was already there. Apurv drove straight to college where both of them were waiting to receive him.

'Dude, what's wrong with your face?' Ritvik asked.

'Long story, fuck it.'

'Did you try to shave for the first time?' Sia asked.

'Is there anything we can hide from girls?' Apurv asked sarcastically.

'I doubt it.'

'Seriously? What the . . .' Ritvik couldn't stop laughing.

Till they reached the party, Apurv was mocked. Friends are often ruthless in such situations. The stage was set and the speakers were already blasting music. It was so loud that they could hardly hear anyone speak. Everyone was grooving to the tunes played by the DJ.

'Amyra has been made Miss Fresher. You missed it,' Ritvik informed both Sia and Apurv who were late.

'You're joking, right?'

'No. Why would I? Aren't you happy?'

Sia was hardly able to hear their conversation because of the music and didn't bother interfering.

'Certainly not. That almost concludes my chances,' Apurv replied in a sad voice.

'Oh crap! Don't worry. I have a solution.'

'A solution?'

'Yes.' Ritvik unzipped his bag and showed him five half-litre bottles of Thums Up. Sia too peeped in, looking puzzled.

'You mean Thums Up is the solution?'

'No, the whisky in it is,' Ritvik winked.

'Are you serious?'

'Of course.'

'I've never had whisky before.' Apurv confessed that he never really had an opportunity to drink before.

'Do you think I am a drunkard? It's my first time too,' Ritvik replied.

'No, guys, please don't.' Sia looked scared.

Sia tried stopping them from drinking on campus but both the guys were convinced that they should go for it. They also saw a couple of other groups drinking which motivated them further. Sip by sip, minute by minute and song after song, they felt tipsier. The more they drank, the more effortlessly their Ganapati *visarjan* dance moves came out. They also became more emotional.

'Sia, you are my best friend. The bestest.'

'Apurv, you should stop it. The two of you are already three bottles down.'

'Don't worry. We still have two more. Sia, I have one question. Did you also get cut when you shaved for the first time?'

Apurv had an innocent look in his drunken eyes as if he seriously wanted an answer.

'No, I never use a razor.'

'Wow, you're so technologically advanced. You should be a techie rather than a designer. Next time, before shaving, I will ask for your kit. It seems safer. You are my best friend.'

Apurv was swaying to the music and that's when Amyra saw Sia standing behind him and waved at her. Sia waved back when she saw Amyra coming towards her. Apurv, who was totally lost, saw Amyra walk towards him all of a sudden.

Is this real? Is time moving in the opposite direction or am I really drunk? Why is she coming towards me again? No headphones? Even her dress is different. She was in jeans but now she is in a dress. Oh fuck, she is coming here for real.

Apurv drank the remaining Thums Up in one go. He stayed quiet while he saw Sia and Amyra interacting.

It was only when Sia turned towards him that he tried to fake a smile as if he was not drunk.

'This is Apurv, my friend,' Sia said as she introduced him to Amyra.

'Hi, Apurv. Nice to meet you.'

'Where are your headphones?' Apurv was still in a trance.

'Aren't you the same guy who was looking for Starbucks today?'

Sia was puzzled and wondered if Amyra too was drunk.

'Yes, I love you. Sia, I love her. I love you too. But I love her more.' Apurv grinned without realizing what he was saying.

'What? You have gone nuts.' Amyra took back the hand that she had extended for a handshake.

'No, seriously, I love you. I have since day one.' Apurv continued to babble.

'He is drunk. I'll catch you later.' Sia was embarrassed by Apurv's behaviour. Amyra walked away without reacting. Sia spent the next few minutes screaming at Apurv. In response, he dared her to drink.

'Come on, have a sip. Break the rules. I dare you.'

'No.'

'You think you don't have guts? You came out of the Blue Whale Challenge alive. You certainly need guts for that. Believe in yourself. Come on,' Apurv urged her.

'You think I can't? Let me show you.'

Sia took a bottle out of the bag and chugged it in one go. Only after she had finished the bottle did she realize that she felt different. Once the whisky entered her system, her control exited. It is said that whisky mixes well with everything apart from the decisions we take when drunk. Sia even accepted Apurv's dare to go on stage and talk about everyone who had insulted her.

As she walked towards the stage, she felt like she had superpowers. Without worrying about the consequences, she snatched the mic from the host and unplugged the speakers to stop the music. Ritvik who had gone to the bathroom and missed all the drama returned just in time and stood beside Apurv. He hadn't expected his ten minutes in the bathroom to be so eventful. After looking at Apurv once, Sia exploded.

'To all those who think I am fat and ugly, you need to "FOCUS". Yes, you need to Fuck Off Cause You are Shit. Get the hell out of here, you rascals. You wrote shit about me on the blackboard, I shit on your face, you assholes. Talk to my middle finger.'

As she got off the stage, Apurv and Ritvik were waiting for her. The three of them ran away from the campus. Apurv even forgot his Vespa. They weren't aware of anything they had done that evening. Apurv had just confessed his love to Amyra without caring about her response. They had all got drunk for the first time ever. And Sia had kicked the balls of all her bullies publicly.

Sometimes you meet people and it's clear that you belong together. Out of nowhere, these people come into your life and make you feel alive. Apurv was one such person in Sia's life. The girl who had no reason to live had not only attacked her haters that night, but also broken the rules by drinking on the campus. All within a week of making this new friend.

Follow Your Brain, the Heart
Is an Idiot

Arelationship works best when the people in it grow and become better in each other's company. Ritvik, Sia and Apurv's bond kept growing stronger as they spent more time with each other. They could spend hours together without getting bored. They could also share secrets without being judged. Sia received some much-needed undivided attention in the company of these guys. She was enjoying this new phase of her life.

All three of them were shortlisted for the play. The day the announcements were made, they had to audition for the final selection. Apurv submitted his write-up and left early because it was his mother's birthday. Ritvik and Sia had just auditioned for the voice-over.

'Sia, can we go out to eat something? I am hungry,' Ritvik requested.

'Now?'

'Ya. Let's go to Growel's. It's within walking distance.'

Ritvik was not really hungry, but for the last few days he had wanted to make a confession. Every day he thought he would speak out but something or the other stopped him from doing so. He thought he had the perfect opportunity to speak his heart out that day because he needed to be alone with her to help her understand the lab incident. He could have deleted the incident from his mind because Sia had no clue he was the one who had sketched her, but his conscience killed him every day.

'What do you plan to do after college?' Sia asked Ritvik on their way to the restaurant.

'I don't know. I just took science because my parents thought I would look like a fool if I opted for commerce or arts after getting more than 90 per cent.'

'What silly notions we have. I wonder if anyone takes science because they want to.'

'Yes, people like Apurv do. He should have taken commerce; his wish of finding a girlfriend would have been fulfilled by now.'

Sia grinned as they entered the restaurant and took a seat. After ordering snacks and replying to pending WhatsApp messages, Ritvik finally decided to speak.

His trembling hands, beating heart and shaky legs clearly revealed his nervousness.

'Sia, I want to tell you something. I don't know how you will take it but trust me, I never wanted or expected what happened,' Ritvik said in a low voice.

'What do you mean? Are you okay? Do you want some Thums Up?' Sia sensed his nervousness and tried to lighten the mood.

'I am serious.'

Sia looked straight into his eyes when she realized the intensity of the situation.

'Do you remember the chemistry lab incident?'

'Of course, how can I forget?' she responded in anger as the memories flashed in her mind.

'I was the one who had initially made the drawing of you. But it was because I wanted you to realize that you aren't ugly but chubby and cute. My intention was to make you smile. I didn't realize the extent to which our classmates would go. I just left class for some work and the drama unfolded. Please forgive me.'

Sia stayed silent for some time and then spoke.

'Why are you telling me this now? I mean I didn't even know about it and was actually over that incident.' Sia had tears in her eyes.

'I felt like I should tell you. We are always together in college and I had been hiding this from you. I felt it wasn't right.'

'And was it right to express concern over my looks?'

'No. But I realized that later. I wish I was mature enough to understand it before,' Ritvik tried to defend himself.

'Was Apurv also involved in it?'

'No, he didn't even know you that time. I know you are close to Apurv now but I have only the two of you. You both mean a lot to me, although I've never said this before.'

Ritvik really cared for his friends and couldn't think of hurting them intentionally. Sia realized this and knew that his actions weren't intentional. But that incident had affected her deeply. She felt broken. She was angry that he had stayed tight-lipped over the past few days.'

'You hurt me, Ritvik. Goodbye.'

Without letting him respond, Sia walked away. Ritvik ran behind her but she refused to look back.

'Please forgive me.'

'Leave me alone for now.'

Neither words nor tears can describe how a broken heart feels. He watched her leave and the worst part was that he felt like he deserved it. The moment she walked away, he felt a part of him leave, something he had never felt before. Had he started falling for her? He had always thought that she was just a friend. But 'just friends' don't look at each other like that.

He immediately sent her a message.

I feel ashamed that I broke your trust. I'm sorry. There is nothing in the whole world that I will allow to come between us—not even my own mistakes. Please try to understand. If I had done it deliberately, I would have hurt you when we became friends, but I was just waiting to tell you the truth. Doesn't that prove that I can never hurt you? Please, let it go.

Sia was already on her way home when she responded.

Ritvik, can you please leave me alone for some time? I understand that you didn't do it on purpose but even I have emotions. I just need some time.

Ritvik didn't react further. He thought it was better to give Sia some space. The real problem is that we get attached. And once we're attached to someone, we do everything we can to please them. Sia was hurt and Ritvik was ready to do anything to make her smile.

'You look disturbed. Don't you want to take part in the play?' Apurv asked Sia when he saw her sitting alone in a classroom.

'It's not like that. I am just a little upset.'

'Anything specific?'

'I think I should start loving my fat rather than anyone else. It seems to stick to me loyally when everyone else prefers to hurt me and leave.'

'I must say that your sense of humour has improved after being with me for a few days.' Apurv tried to bring a genuine smile to her face. 'You can talk to me.'

Sia told him what had happened the previous afternoon. He clearly remembered every minute of that day and disclosed the truth to her.

'Sia, you have really misunderstood him. Ritvik is a nice chap. We were together in the lab when the incident took place. Before everyone came into the lab, he had made the sketch with no intention to hurt you. I clearly remember he had said that he just wanted to make you smile as he had seen you hating yourself. I was the one who took him away to register for the play and things got messed up. You should blame me instead.'

'Which means Ritvik was not lying yesterday. He said the same thing—that he left for some work and when he returned the drama was over.'

Sia felt guilty for behaving the way she did with Ritvik.

'Exactly! Ritvik would never hurt anyone. He may make some mistakes but his intentions are good. He'll hurt himself to help others but I personally don't think he was wrong. The rest is your call.'

Before Sia could speak, Apurv got a call from Ritvik who soon joined them. He had been looking for Sia who was ignoring his calls. He had planned something to make her feel special, and this time he was a little more careful.

'I am sorry.'

'Oh fuck!' Apurv screamed all of a sudden. Both Sia and Ritvik turned towards him in confusion. 'Now I know why the hell you were apologizing repeatedly when Sia was about to jump. You thought she was doing it because of you.' Apurv couldn't stop laughing.

'Such idiots you are! I am sorry, Ritvik. Apurv told me everything that happened that day. I overreacted.'

'It was my fault and I am making up for it,' Ritvik said while unzipping his bag. He took out a big box of Hershey's chocolates. He had invested all his pocket money in making her smile. And she did!

'How did you know I love these?'

'You're eating these in your latest Instagram video. You looked super cute.'

They hugged each other and Apurv joined in. Things are so simple with friends, unlike in relationships—one day you are upset with them and the next day you are drinking together. That's what makes friendship so pure. The three of them were better together!

'Now let's leave. We are supposed to gather in the seminar room. All the shortlisted students are being called. The final team for the play is supposed to be announced today,' Apurv declared.

All the students had already gathered in the hall by the time they reached. The student who was in charge of the play was announcing the final team. The three of them had been selected and assigned specific roles. Apurv had to write the script along with a couple of other students while Sia and Ritvik had to provide voice-overs for the play. Apurv was not at all surprised as he knew they were the best in the batch. But what came as a surprise to him was the name of the female lead—Amyra!

She entered the hall a few seconds after her name was announced and apologized for coming late. She looked around to see if she knew anyone. The moment her eyes fell on Sia, she came towards her. After congratulating and greeting each other, Amyra glanced at Apurv who stood there paralysed.

'Oh, hi, you seem to follow me everywhere. First Starbucks, then the freshers' party and now here.'

'I think destiny is desperately trying to bring us together, but we seem to screw its plan by not talking to each other.'

'Don't start again.' Amyra thought there was something peculiar about him but before they could interact further, she was called away by the student incharge along with the male lead.

Apurv was flattered but Sia was annoyed.

'Are you following her?' Sia asked in annoyance.

'No, I mean yeah . . . I mean I like her . . . love her. You know, this is something more than a mere crush.'

'And you never bothered to tell me?'

'I didn't know she was your friend. I've never really seen you two together,' Apurv defended himself.

'So you'll only tell me things about your life if I know the people involved? Don't I tell you everything, from my dreams to my fears?'

'Yes, but this was different and we never discussed it before. Why would I hide anything from you? Rather, if I had known you knew her so well, I would have asked you to anchor my love life which is currently floating in a sea of confusion.'

'Stop giving me your fucking metaphors, Mr Writer. Save them for your lead.'

'But you are a voice-over artist. You reveal the feelings of the actors. You are their inner voice. Please tell her my feelings. I will do anything for you. Please. You are my best friend, right?'

'Get lost. I am not doing anything for you.'

'Please Sia,' Apurv called after Sia as she walked away. Ritvik, too, followed Sia as she looked a little upset and he didn't want to leave her alone. Apurv stood there confused about whether he should convince a friend or wait for the person he loved to return. Love won over friendship and he decided to stay back thinking he could convince Sia sooner or later. But he had to make a start with Amyra— it was now or never!

Apurv often stared cluelessly at Amyra, like he did at his homework. And just like his homework, she was a mystery to him. Every now and then he would just find himself staring at her absent-mindedly.

'Where's Sia? Has she disappeared again?' Amyra asked when she returned.

Apurv loved every word she spoke and every movement she made.

It's so easy to interact with your friends because you don't have to think twice about expressing your true self. But with love, it's always the other way.

'I think she wanted to give us privacy. You know, just you and me.'

All Amyra could do was make a wry face.

'So, you write?' Amyra asked as they walked out of the hall.

'I try to.'

'And you just broke up?'

'When did we start dating?'

'Arggh! I asked because these days broken-hearted people write to deal with their frustration.'

'It could be the other way around too. Some write to find love. To get the girl they want,' he said with a wink.

'Trying too hard?'

'No, you haven't really seen me hard. I mean try.'

'You jerk.'

'Okay, on a serious note, would you like to read my work?'

'Sure,' she said casually.

'You need to give me your number for that. I'll WhatsApp it to you.'

'Wow, is this a new trick to ask a girl for her number?'

'No, it's not a trick. I'm trying to be polite. Otherwise I would have taken it from Sia.'

Amyra didn't know how to reply to that.

'Ah! There they are! My lovely friends,' said Apurv as he spotted Ritvik and Sia sitting on a bench.

There was something enigmatic about him that captivated Amyra, a magnetic pull which she couldn't resist. It was like he was hiding something deep within him. Was he trying to hide his true identity? Who was he behind the flowery words he spoke? The deeper she looked into his eyes, the more she wanted to understand him. His mysterious looks reflected a profound innocence of which even he was unaware.

When Amyra gave him her number, Apurv was transported to another galaxy. He was sure it would be a long time before he got her number. But it all happened in the blink of an eye. Love is a complicated thing, and you're never quite sure how things will turn out. You just have to wait patiently for someone special to come your way and make you happy.

Don't Mess with My BFF

'Were you stalking her?' Sia asked Apurv once again after Amyra had left.

'Stalking is such a strong word. I was just conducting intense research on her.'

'Don't act smart. You aren't, for your information.'

'I thought the same thing, but guess what? She gave me her number. Now I feel otherwise. She looked gorgeous in her Indian attire today.' Apurv felt like he had won a gold medal in the Olympics.

'She won't be able to handle you anyway.'

Ritvik was enjoying the drama from the sidelines. He could see that Sia was a little jealous, not because she had a problem with Apurv having a girlfriend, but because she wanted him to love her more. She didn't mind him calling someone else beautiful, but she just wanted him to give her more attention. She didn't mind him talking to someone else for hours, she just wanted him to handle her when she had mood swings. Apurv succeeded in making her feel better with his antics as they headed to the chemistry lab for their next class.

It was Apurv's first time in that class and the professor stared at him as he entered.

'Are you a part of this class?'

'Yes, Sir, but I couldn't attend the last three times. My *nana* has chemotherapy sessions on Mondays. Now that my dad is back in town, he'll be able to look after him.'

'Stop giving me lame excuses.' The professor could sense that Apurv was lying. After all, he was a professor: they know everything even though they act like they don't.

Amyra followed Apurv as it was her first class as well. However, this time the professor didn't comment on her attire. She was dressed in a salwar kurta, pretending to be someone she was not, just like she did with her relatives. Once the class started, they were instructed to follow the steps in the textbook and show the professor the result of the experiment. Apurv, however, was preparing himself to follow the steps in the textbook of love and get a result out of Amyra. He texted her.

Now I don't have to check your last seen on WhatsApp. At least for two hours.

When she saw his message, Amyra looked straight at him. She saw that he was staring at her, mesmerized by her beauty.

Why?
Why would I need to? I can see you right here in front of my eyes.

Apurv grinned as Amyra tried to hide behind her hair.

Do you think you're funny?
I caught you smiling. For guys like me, WhatsApp is the only medium through which we can express our emotions.
What do you mean guys like you?
Guys who cannot go beyond asking directions to Starbucks ☺

He had finally confessed but Amyra wasn't upset. She replied with a laughing emoji.

What Apurv loved the most about the chemistry lab was that he could spend time with Amyra. Those secret glances made the class more interesting.

Sia saw them stealing glances at each other, witnessing their silent love story. She texted Apurv.

Anyone can see what's going on between you two. Concentrate on the concentrated acid in the tube, else it will burn your ass.

Still chatting with Amyra, he replied to Sia's message, not realizing it was her.

Do you think we should ditch maths class and go for a movie?
I wish I had a loaded gun right now.

Sia was burning with anger.

Apurv realized what he had done and burst out laughing. After a few seconds, Sia joined in. Apurv created a WhatsApp group including the four of them and finalized the plan for the movie. Ritvik agreed and Amyra too didn't have a problem. She was fascinated by him, although she didn't show it. Apurv, in turn, was confused because of the mixed signals she was sending him. It was getting harder for him to pretend to be just friends because he wanted her every time he looked at her. He kept wondering what was on her mind. Were they just friends? But 'just friends' don't look at each other like they did!

You don't know how I feel, always longing for your attention. I want to talk to you every day, every minute and every second. You don't know how just talking to you makes me feel complete. Most of all you don't know how much you mean to me, he thought as he looked at Amyra from the corner of his eye as they walked towards the campus gate.

They decided to go to the movie theatre in a cab. Apurv would pick up his Vespa later. Amyra was about to book the cab when she got a call and excused herself.

'Sia, will you sit in the front? I want to sit with Amyra. Please understand,' Apurv requested, taking advantage of Amyra's absence.

Although he didn't mean to, he was hurting Sia and she felt unwanted once again. Ritvik could sense this in the way she chose to remain silent, not knowing how to respond.

'Don't worry, you enjoy sitting with both the girls, I will sit in the front.'

'Ah! A threesome. I don't mind,' Apurv joked.

'Your jokes are getting repetitive day by day. Stop trying so hard.'

Sia wanted to warn him about how Amyra had abandoned her friends in school. But she didn't know if she was genuinely concerned for him or if she was jealous. Before she could get her thoughts in order, Amyra returned.

'I am so sorry, guys, I have to leave.' She looked upset.

'What happened?' Apurv looked even more upset.

'I forgot it's my sister's birthday today. She had asked me to bring snacks in the morning for the party. If I go for the movie now, I'll be late and her party will be ruined.'

'You are lying. How could you forget your sister's birthday when you wished her in the morning and promised to bring the snacks?' Sia blurted out.

'No, trust me,' Amyra said looking at Apurv.

'I don't know how I forgot but this happens to me often. It's not the first time. Don't you remember I forgot about the chemistry practical even after you had reminded me?'

'This is strange. Only kids are this careless. The tickets have already been booked.' Sia was extremely frustrated. But somewhere inside, she felt a sense of relief because she wasn't wrong about Amyra. Also, now she could spend some time with Apurv without worrying about how Amyra felt. But her happiness didn't last long because Apurv broke the awkward silence.

'It's okay. We will go some other time. I'll drop you. At least then you will get there early.'

Sia didn't feel bad because Apurv decided to drop Amyra, but because he didn't even say a word to her for dropping out at the last moment. Amyra apologized again before going with Apurv. In the middle of all this mess the only person who was genuinely happy was Ritvik. He finally had some time alone with Sia. He wanted to be with her and understand whether he liked her as a friend or if there was something more to their relationship. However, he also realized that he had to cage his feelings because he sensed that Sia loved Apurv. The way she reacted over the entire Amyra episode made his belief firmer. But rather than stressing over things, he preferred to live for the moment. He decided to enjoy the time he had with her.

Even after they had left, Sia continued to bitch about Amyra. 'I am sure she is lying. She must have got a call from some boyfriend. You know she had a boyfriend in school. She was always fast for her age, you see.'

Ritvik thought it prudent not to say anything.

For a moment, Sia even thought that Apurv and Amyra had purposely planned this so they could go on a date together. But she felt ashamed for thinking this way because she knew Apurv would never stoop to this level.

'I feel we should carry on. Why should we miss the movie because of them?' Ritvik looked at Sia, wondering if she was comfortable being alone with him.

'I think you are right. Why should we screw up our day because of them? Let's book a cab.'

Ritvik was on a high because it was not often that he went to watch a movie alone with a girl. Although it was not an official date, he decided to have the popcorn that he loved and buy her the samosa that he knew she was crazy about.

'Have you ever had a girlfriend?' Sia asked as she sat next to him in the back of the cab.

'No, but there was a girl I liked a lot in ninth grade.'

'What happened?'

'Nothing. She hooked up with someone else. My grades were affected because I thought my life was over without her. It felt like no one would come into my life ever again. It was as if the world stopped spinning and I locked myself in a shell. But time heals everything. Days turned into months and I found that the world never stopped. Rather, it was I who stopped. I was the one who stopped trying to live. After my board exams, I stood up again. And here I am now, happy and complete,' Ritvik smiled.

'Wow! How easily you've defined life.' Sia held his hand casually.

'I wish it were as easy as I make it seem,' Ritvik muttered looking at their hands locked together. He got an adrenaline rush the moment she held his hand. 'You know what? You are one of a kind, so different from everyone else. You've become an important part of my life. No other friendship has made me feel this way.'

'Aww, that's so sweet of you. But trust me, I never thought we would sit together in the back of a cab and go for a movie when I met you for the first time. Thanks for all that you have done for me. My life revolves around you and Apurv. I would feel like the Thakur in *Sholay* without you guys. Both my hands chopped off. My Jai and Veeru.'

'Let him be Jai. I don't want to die at the end of our story,' Ritvik winked.

'Asshole.' She tightened her grip on his hand, unknowingly making his heart skip a beat.

'I am sorry for backing out at the last moment. Don't misunderstand me,' Amyra apologized as they drove towards her house.

'For me, this is no less than a movie. You are the first girl to sit on my Vespa.' Apurv looked at her in the rear-view mirror. He blushed when he realized that she was looking at him too.

'Liar.' She pinched his arm and he somehow managed to control his Vespa.

'What? It's the truth! I mean, Sia has, but with you it's different.'

'Different in what sense?' The gentle breeze made her look irresistible.

'You don't know?'

'No, I don't.'

'Okay, then let it be a secret.'

They looked at each other shyly in the silence that followed.

'I remember you telling me some time back that you stay in Versova. So why are we going to Andheri?'

'No, I stay in Andheri.'

'Oh! Maybe I misunderstood.'

Seconds later, she took him by surprise and wrapped her arms around him. She rested her chin on his shoulder, driving him crazy. But, at the same time, everything felt just right. Her tickling breath on his ears made him freeze. Somehow, he managed to drop her off and drive back home. He wanted to park in a corner and kiss her. This, however, remained a distant fantasy, one he never thought would come true. But her first touch spoke volumes.

I just reached home.

Apurv received a message from Amyra as he entered his house.

Now? I dropped you off a while back.
Oops. The message got delivered late. Network issues. Anyway, I am waiting to read what you've written. ♥

It seemed like her touch was fire because it melted him completely. He was still blushing, thinking about those moments with her. Your first love stays with you forever. Apurv compiled all his writing and thought of sending it to her. He indirectly wanted to convey his feelings through it. If anything went wrong, he could hide behind the claim that it was fiction.

He finally got the courage to send her his work.

Sometimes you open yourself up to a person because you feel and believe that they are different, and maybe this time they won't break your heart and that your love will be requited. You just lose yourself in love and in the thought of being loved.

But the worst part is that nothing is guaranteed. There's no guarantee on how long you'll be with them. You're not guaranteed complete happiness and you're not guaranteed that things will be perfect. You just have to have faith. You'll never know how to love someone wholeheartedly if you haven't been hurt before. You have to turn your heartbreak into something positive and make the most of your situation. That's how you have to be your own inspiration. To live with the person who puts you before them and to be loved by the person who treats you like no one else!

Amyra soon replied to the write-up that Apurv had sent.

Wow, I was actually lost in it as if I wanted more.

He was disappointed because he had expected something more than a one-line response. But she had other plans. Apurv wrote:

I keep thinking of how much I love talking to you, how good you look when you smile, how much I love your silly jokes. I catch myself smiling every time you give me that look. I wonder what will happen the next time we're together. You're special.

He wanted to send kiss emojis but decided against it. After thinking for a while, he wrote the four words that expressed his feelings for her.

You are no less.

Apurv felt like he was totally submerged in love. He wanted her to be his romantic novel, to allow him to turn the pages to know the depth of her thoughts. But she happened to be a thriller, always keeping him on the edge and haunting him because he never knew what was coming next.

My Feelings? Oh, Don't You Worry!

Two months later:
Relationships are unpredictable as most of the time you are thrown into situations that are absolutely unfamiliar. Apurv, too, was in a fix as even the thought of being friends with Amyra never crossed his mind. He had finally stopped spending time on Tinder. Although he appeared on all Amyra's stories, he still wasn't a part of her life. Amyra was dazzled by Apurv but she didn't commit to a relationship.

Sia's relationship with herself had begun the day she stopped being harsh on herself and paid more attention to the voices on the inside rather than those on the outside. She had feelings for Ritvik but she never displayed them. Ritvik, too, waited for the right time to reveal how he felt. As far as Apurv was concerned,

Sia was hurt because his attention had been divided, making their relationship vulnerable.

Even on the day the script for the play was finalized, Sia looked upset. This wasn't because of external factors but because she had to fight her inner struggle once again. The team had decided to celebrate at the Sky Deck Lounge, but Sia was in no mood to go. She attracted unwanted stares at such places which disturbed her and made her want to avoid them. She was only considering going because Apurv and Amyra were going together and she didn't want Ritvik to be alone.

'Sia, I'll be there with you. If someone says anything I will fuck them up. Also, let me tell you again, you're not fat, you're beautiful. Don't fool yourself by thinking you have to fit a certain mould to be loved and appreciated. There is a guy out there who will celebrate you for exactly who you are.'

'Why don't you understand? I don't know how to dance, and even if I did, I'd look ridiculous because of my body.'

'Who is asking you to dance? You can just sit with a chilled glass of beer or a Coke. I'll be your dance partner if you want. We will make a pathetic pair because even I can't dance.'

'Shut up. I won't mind dancing with you but I'm afraid of what other people might say.'

'Then come along. You're not a delicate flower, you are a real girl and real girls don't shy away.'

'Fine, I'll come just for you.'

Apurv, too, had tried convincing her in his own way but she knew Amyra would accompany him and it would hardly matter. It wasn't as if she had started hating him. She still cared, probably a lot more than she let on. It was out of concern for him that she didn't accept his closeness with Amyra because she remembered what Amyra had been like in school.

'How did you get here? I was calling you continuously. Didn't you check your phone?' Apurv questioned Sia as she entered with Ritvik.

Apurv and Amyra had already been there for half an hour.

'Oh sorry, I was on the bike with Ritvik.'

'Excuse me, I'll get the drinks.' Ritvik walked towards the bar leaving Apurv and Sia alone.

This was the first time at a lounge for both Apurv and Sia. But instead of being excited they sat in awkward silence because they hadn't talked to each other candidly in a long time. Sia could not even remember when she had last expressed herself to Apurv without thinking about Amyra. They both sensed that something was wrong. They hardly knew what was going on in each other's lives but still pretended to be best friends.

'Remember when all of us used to arrive at places together?' Sia's grief was evident in her voice.

'We are still together.'

'We aren't.' Sia looked at him but turned away after a few seconds.

'Nothing can separate best friends.'

'Ask yourself, are we still best friends? When was the last time you asked me how I felt? What was happening in my life?'

'Of course we are. I was just—I don't know how to say it. I really love Amyra.'

'Does that give you the right to ignore your friends and love them less?' Sia summed up the last couple of months in a single question. Friends can break your heart too and it hurts more than anything else in the world. She felt like she was walking past her best friend, pretending that she didn't know him. The damage was done.

Ritvik got drinks for Apurv and himself to raise a toast along with the entire team. Once the entire cast and crew of the play had arrived, everyone raised a toast to the rehearsals that were supposed to start next week. Amyra snatched the drink from Apurv and smiled widely, surprising everyone.

'It's my turn today,' she teased him.

'I beg your pardon?' Apurv couldn't comprehend what she was trying to suggest.

'How could you forget? You snatched my coffee in the canteen which burnt your tongue, Mr Writer.'

'Oh damn! Yeah. But trust me, that was not part of any game. It just happened.' After a couple of drinks, everyone was high and dancing. The four of them were seated away from the rest of the group and talking casually about their college life when Amyra's question made everyone laugh, including Sia.

'Have you ever forgotten your way home?'

Ritvik somehow controlled his laughter. 'Yeah, the time I was drunk at the freshers' party.'

'Don't drink too much and you won't land up at your neighbours' house while they are making out,' Apurv chimed in.

'Have you spoken to Pihu from school recently?' Sia asked Amyra, trying to make conversation.

But that didn't go too well because she responded in a sad tone. 'I don't want to talk about our school friends.'

No one raised the question again and they decided just to have fun. Another drink later and both Apurv and Amyra were on the dance floor. Ritvik asked Sia to dance but she turned him down. She preferred to spend time talking to Ritvik alone. When the DJ started playing soft music, Apurv became a little uncomfortable as he had never danced to slow music before.

'I've never done this,' he confessed as they stood extremely close to each other.

'What?' Amyra looked surprised.

'I know it's lame.' Apurv let out a small laugh. 'Amyra, will you be my first dance partner?' His voice cracked at the word 'dance'.

Amyra blushed and nodded. She did everything she could to keep the huge grin off her face, but she failed.

'Okay, do you want me to show you what to do?'

Apurv nodded again. Amyra gently lifted his arms and placed them around her waist while she put her arms around his neck. She stepped a bit closer and slowly started to sway to the music. It didn't take long for Apurv to get comfortable. It didn't seem possible for them to get closer but they did. They stole subtle glances at each other's eyes and lips. Apurv pulled Amyra closer and squeezed her lightly. Amyra was already drunk and every touch made her weak. The heat in her body made her surrender.

Apurv leaned in slowly. 'Should we stay here?'

'Let's go somewhere else.'

They escaped from the crowd when no one was watching. Ritvik and Sia were busy discussing something, making it easier.

Before they knew it, their tongues fell in love. They were in an underground parking lot which was thankfully secluded.

'It's my first time,' Apurv said nervously.

Amyra turned pink at the unexpected confession and the butterflies in her stomach went wild.

'Isn't that supposed to be my line?' She glanced around to see if anyone was watching.

'You have never kissed before? But you had a boyfriend.' Apurv had his fingers crossed. He wanted to be her first kiss. His eyes looked innocent as he desperately waited for her to say yes.

'Yeah, but I was in school.'

He touched her hair and took a stray strand in his fingers, placing it behind her ear as he moved closer.

She gasped a little.

'What's wrong?'

'I'm sorry. It's just that you make me really nervous.'

'But you do want me to kiss you?' he asked her, just to be sure. Her eyes glanced at his lips and she gave him such a small nod that he barely noticed. Leaning against a pillar, she waited patiently with her eyes closed. Apurv could feel her breath. The cars in the parking lot were witness to their first kiss.

When he finally pulled away, he kept his face close to hers. He felt her breath change from rapid to steady as if the kiss had a calming effect on her. He opened his eyes to see hers closed with her mouth slightly open. She looked dazed with her flushed cheeks, making him want to kiss her again. He brought his face as close as possible with their noses rubbing against each other.

'May I kiss you again?'

'Please.' With one word she melted his heart and he kissed her again. It felt like he was falling. The caress of her lips seemed much softer than his. Soon, she let out a moan, feeling desire run from her heart to her chest and further down. His finger touched her neck, giving her the chills. She felt safe. After taking a deep breath, he bit her gently. It didn't hurt, it only made her want him more. For her, his eyes exuded love, protection, security, safety, patience and respect. They were so lost in each other that they didn't sense someone coming. They didn't hear any footsteps or voices until they heard Sia scream.

'What the fuck are you guys doing?'

She didn't expect to find him there and was visibly shocked. She had thought of walking towards the parking lot exit while Ritvik got his bike out. She was taken aback when she saw Apurv and Amyra caught in a lip-lock. They broke apart as soon as they heard Sia's voice and looked embarrassed. Amyra couldn't even look at Sia.

Sia felt disgusted at seeing her best friend kissing her other friend. She knew she shouldn't be shocked but she felt like everything was going too fast. Annoyed by their intimacy, she walked to the exit without saying a word. Apurv told Amyra to wait near his Vespa and ran behind Sia, but she had already reached the exit. Somehow, even in his drunken state, Apurv was able to catch hold of her. For a few seconds, they stood face-to-face.

'What's wrong with you, Sia? Why are you behaving like a crazy person?'

'What's wrong with me? You should look at yourself!'

'I like her and she likes me. We kissed. Big deal.'

'Of course it is. You just left without informing us. Does falling in love come at the cost of losing friends? Has she even committed herself to you? Are you in a relationship? She is not the right one for you. She never was. And I am not saying this because I am annoyed at you. Yes, I am, but that's a different story altogether.'

'Please stop judging others. I didn't expect this from someone who knows how it feels to be judged. She is not how you think she is. And what story are you talking about? Tell me, once and for all.'

'You only care about her, Apurv. Every time we meet, it's only Amyra that you talk about. What about me? My feelings, my problems, my happiness and my life? In a very short span of time, we became best friends who shared each and every thing. I opened the book of my life to you and this is how you treat me? I have no problem with you making out with anyone because it's your life but my problem is with the way you behave with us. Ritvik hardly cares because he has other friends. What about me? If you had to do this eventually, why did you save me? Do you even know what is happening in my life? When was the last time we really talked? She took my seat on your Vespa. In the last two months, our interactions have stopped. And you say that we are still best friends.'

'Oh, so you are annoyed because I pick her up and drop her off?'

'That's all you have to say? Even cab drivers pick up and drop people. But if expecting you to talk to me is wrong, then maybe you are right.'

'You are just overreacting, Sia. I never ignored you intentionally. Why would I? It's just that I love talking to her and it comes naturally. Also, just because I'm spending time with her doesn't mean I am not friends with you. I do care about you and I still love to be with you like I used to.'

The two best friends were drifting apart. The worst part was that they both actually cared for each other but were not able to hold on to it. Apurv couldn't stop expressing his emotions for Amyra every time he met Sia, while she was suppressing her feelings. Their relationship wasn't complicated, it was just the situation they were in. It's never easy to balance your love life and friendship.

Ritvik brought his bike to where Apurv and Sia were. He was confused by the way they were looking at each other. Sia signalled Ritvik to bring his bike near where she was waiting so they could leave. Although Ritvik was unaware of what had happened, he could sense the tension in the air. Apurv didn't want to hurt Amyra, so he walked towards her and reassured her that everything was fine. He didn't want to ruin the memory of their first kiss. On the one hand, his love life had started moving on the right track, while on the other his friendship was going off the tracks.

Not Sad, but Ain't Happy Either

Sometimes we expect a lot from others because we are willing to do that much for them. Sia had a heavy heart because Apurv was the only friend, apart from Ritvik, for whom she was ready to sacrifice anything.

Ritvik was trying to cement the cracks that had developed in their friendship.

After leaving the lounge, he took her to his favourite Prithvi Cafe where he went whenever he felt low. Sia narrated what had actually happened in the parking lot.

Ritvik would sit at the cafe for hours, sipping on multiple cups of cutting chai. As usual, it was overcrowded and they had to wait for a seat.

'How do you relax in such a crowded place?'

'Why? Should one relax only in bed or while looking at the sea? I feel good when I see so many people around me, discussing their work, their problems, cribbing about life. It makes me feel my life is far better than theirs. Sometimes, I feel insecure too when I see extremely happy faces, but I calm down whenever I look at that man.'

'Which man?'

'Shashi Kapoor, the famous actor. This cafe is owned by the Kapoor family and you often find him here in a wheelchair with his caretaker. He can't speak or recognize people. He just looks at you with a blank face. He was once one of the most popular actors. Now very few people recognize him. Doesn't that complete the circle of life?'

The waiter interrupted their discussion to tell them that their table was ready.

Sia found herself looking at Ritvik from time to time. She had clearly understood his intention and what he'd wanted to convey. She decided to take things easy while spending time with him. That night, as she looked at Ritvik, Sia saw a different side of him. She realized that she liked Ritvik, not because he was a stud but because of the way he always stood by her. Or was it because she could see Ritvik's hidden feelings in his eyes?

'We decide to give up on life and relationships so easily. Just try being in his shoes for once. Imagine what this man must feel now. Do you think Apurv kissing Amyra is such a big problem that you would end your friendship with him?'

'I don't know.'

'You are his friend and she is his girlfriend. Obviously, he will treat her differently.'

'She isn't. At least not yet. They are hanging somewhere in between and I am sure she won't commit to him.'

'Whatever. You should not take such things to heart.'

'It's easy for you to say that.'

'Why? You're constantly repeating the same things about Apurv whenever we meet. Do I get insecure? Of course not, I understand that he is a part of your life, and I don't mind that even though I like you. For me, it's your company that matters.'

'You like me?'

Ritvik had hesitated to reveal his feelings but now that the secret was out, he decided to go with the flow. He wasn't scared because he didn't expect her to feel the same way.

'I do, but you love Apurv and that's okay.'

'I don't love him. I mean I do. But not like that. He is a friend. I just expected him to understand my feelings.'

'You don't love him?' Ritvik was astonished as well. He couldn't have been more delighted.

'Of course not.'

'I always thought you did.'

'I had no clue you liked me.' Sia blushed and Ritvik smiled. No words were exchanged but their hearts connected.

In that moment they knew that it was time to start something new, a new togetherness, and trust the magic of a new beginning.

Amyra was like a gentle breeze, lightly tapping, softly rapping, at the door to Apurv's heart. Once Sia and Ritvik left, Apurv and Amyra walked back towards his Vespa, still lingering over their first kiss and tipsy with the unfulfilled desires burning inside them. While in one corner of his heart he felt dejected at the way Sia had left, he also felt ecstatic thinking about the moment when he had held Amyra close.

But one look at Amyra and he knew that she had consumed far too much alcohol that evening. 'Are you okay?'

'It felt awesome.' Amyra blushed, and Apurv couldn't resist holding her hand. Wasting no time at all, Apurv pressed his lips against hers, literally taking her breath away. He was much more confident this time.

'Let's do something we shouldn't be doing. Fuck, Amyra, let me take you back to my place, please?' He growled while staring intently at her. She too looked at him, desperately trying to focus on the question at hand.

Fuck, no! Say no, Amyra. Say no right now. She simply replied with a nod because she had lost the ability to speak. Amyra concentrated on the rhythm of Apurv's lips working against hers. Then he suddenly broke the kiss and started his Vespa.

'Don't worry, Amyra, it won't be long now,' he whispered into her ear, causing a shiver to run down her body.

I can't wait to have him. After what felt like forever, they finally pulled up to Apurv's apartment. His parents were away and he was taking full advantage of that. The security guard looked at them in shock but they ignored him. They ran up to the fourth floor and Apurv made sure his neighbours' door was locked. He quickly reached into his back pocket, and pulled out the keys, struggling to unlock the door.

'Apurv, hurry the fuck up,' she whispered, scared of getting caught. He replied with a simple grunt before the door finally swung open. Once inside, he closed the door with a kick and instantly pushed Amyra against it.

'Apurv.'

He held her wrists gently. He looked pained. 'Don't.'

'What?'

'I won't be able to control myself if you say my name like that again.' He groaned lightly. 'I've never wanted someone so much,' he said in a low, husky voice.

'I need you now, Apurv.' His masculine scent tantalized her. She unknowingly pressed her body against his, ready to lose her V-card.

'I love the way you say my name,' he sighed. 'You are so beautiful. When I saw you in college I never thought my first time would be with you.'

Adrenaline rushed through her body and all traces of tipsiness were gone. All she could think about was Apurv, his body pinning her beneath him. She was soothed by his embrace and relaxed against his body. He, in turn, forgot about his past and future and was reduced to this moment with her. They were together in an elemental embrace.

When it was all over, he pulled out. She hadn't reached any mountain high or felt herself exploding, at least not like he had. It was all over his face, relaxed and at peace. *How easy it is for men*, she thought.

'I love you,' Apurv whispered as he lay on his back with his face tilted towards her.

Amyra just stared at him; no doubt he had made her first time memorable but the more Apurv tried to express his true love, the more she restrained her emotions. Apurv didn't stress over it because their affection was real.

'I'm going to shower. Do you want to join me?' Apurv winked as he got out of bed.

'No. You carry on.' Amyra pulled the bed sheet to cover herself.

Amyra had other plans in mind. Once Apurv went into the bathroom, she removed the slab of Cadbury from her bag and melted it in the microwave. She took the bowl and a spoon and entered the bedroom with the sheet still wrapped around her. All set, she waited for Apurv to come out. The moment he did, he was instantly turned on at the sight of her on the bed, wrapped only in a thin sheet, her thighs bare. God, the hot chocolate was equally tempting. He just couldn't take his eyes off it. She dipped the spoon in the chocolate and licked it clean while moaning with lust.

As she took another spoonful, she started to remove the sheet. Her soft skin shone, making Apurv lose his composure. With her eyes closed, she slowly ate the chocolate. It was marvellous to watch her eat, except the word 'eat' sounded too indelicate. While she ate, he starved for her and the bed sheet parted slowly to allow him one more trip to heaven.

The canteen was quiet when Amyra entered but Sia was sitting at her usual table. She slapped a self-deprecating smirk on her face although she knew that she was only doing so because it was expected of her.

'Are you okay?' Amyra asked Sia referring to the scene at the lounge a couple of nights ago.

'Am I expected to answer that?'

'No.' Amyra rubbed her hands, looking around to see if she could spot anyone she knew.

Things didn't seem like before. Amyra could see the tension and awkwardness in Sia's eyes but she wanted her to talk about it. She had no hard feelings for Sia. 'Do you know what happened once you left?' Amyra asked Sia. 'We went to his house and did it for the first time. It was heavenly. I never thought he would be so good.' Amyra blushed.

Initially Sia didn't believe her and thought she was spicing up a story. But a few details later Sia realized that she was telling the truth.

'Are you nuts? You lost your virginity? That's shameful.'

'What's so shameful about it? It's not losing anything. Why do we consider our first experiences of everything else to be about gaining something but with sex, for some reason, we magically lose something. I didn't suddenly become impure. I am still the same girl I was. I simply gained experience. This entire concept of virginity is bullshit.'

'Of course, a slut like you would feel indifferently towards sex. Kissing Ishaan at the age of fourteen, wearing short skirts to lure boys and having sex with Apurv at sixteen. From school washrooms to guys' bedrooms. What next? A baby at eighteen?'

Sia was angry because Apurv hadn't told her a thing even though they had talked on the phone. It didn't really matter to her if Apurv and Amyra had sex. Her words had shocked Amyra who didn't expect them from someone who was always mocked for her looks. However, her words were not meant to hurt Amyra, rather they expressed concern for Apurv. What Sia didn't realize was that her approach was absolutely wrong.

Rather than digging deeper to identify the root of her unresolved conflicts, Sia went ahead and attacked Amyra. How easily we criticize someone's way of living when we are unable to articulate our feelings. She is drinking therefore she's a slut. Look at her clothes, she's a whore. She's friends with so many guys, she's a 'ho'. We often prefer to take the easy route of abusing someone when we are upset, and Sia did just that.

'Are you his girlfriend? I wouldn't mind if you were committed to him but girls like you hop from one guy to another and fulfil your desires. You ditched Ishaan in school and I am sure you will ditch Apurv too. You are nothing but a whore.'

That was it. Amyra gave it back to Sia in a manner that was far worse.

'Sia, you've gone way too far. I've never judged you but that hasn't stopped you from judging me. Enough is enough. You think you can judge me just because I slept with him? It's my decision. Who are you to tell me to commit? You are not my mom. Don't act like a jealous bitch just because I can wear short skirts and you can't because you look fat. And don't call me a slut just because no one kissed you when you were fourteen. Did I call you a loser because you haven't slept with anyone yet? You hang out with Ritvik all the time and you guys went out that night as well. Did I assume that you kissed him? How is it possible that he didn't touch you even once?'

'Ritvik is a decent guy. He is not like you, always thinking about sex. Even Apurv was like that before he met you. He was my best friend.'

'What rubbish! Just because Apurv and I enjoy each other's company and spend time with each other doesn't mean we should be committed. Whatever happened that night was mutual and happened in the heat of the moment. No one regrets it but that doesn't mean we should name our relationship. Stop being so judgemental. Instead be happy that I am not going to tell Apurv anything because I am not childish like you. Don't just become fat, become smarter too.'

Sia picked up her bag and walked out of the canteen. All lines had been crossed as Sia and Amyra forgot they were friends. It's saddening how easily the words 'fat' and 'slut' rolled off their tongues. And it's amazing how much meaning is tied to these small words, how badly they can hurt us. It was as if Sia was insecure because of the grudge she held against Amyra since their schooldays. She hated Amyra for befriending everyone except her. Would she be able to become friends with Amyra ever again? Would Apurv continue to be friends with Sia after this incident? One thing was certain: things wouldn't be the same any more.

To Me, You're Perfect

Sometimes two people fall apart for no specific reason. There is no betrayal, no back-stabbing and no distrust. Just a few sharp words are enough to hurt their egos. Sia and Amyra were falling apart, but Amyra had made her realize the importance of love. Where she showed concern for Apurv as she valued his friendship, she unknowingly took Ritvik for granted. He never made her feel alone when he was with her—isn't that the law of a relationship? Also, he never took advantage of her trust when they were alone—isn't that love? Instead of being pissed off about her fight with Amyra, Sia couldn't stop herself from thinking about Ritvik.

Ritvik was about to reach college when he got a text from Sia asking where he was, which made him smile. That day, when he met Sia, he could see the same feeling in her eyes too, something he hadn't seen before.

'You are smiling again. Is everything sorted with Apurv?'

'No. In fact, I had a huge fight with Amyra, but I feel strangely relaxed after it. Also, I've realized that it's better not to stress over what's lost. I should think about those who are valuable. Of course, Apurv is also valuable but I think I am just overthinking things.'

'Oh wow. So it took Amyra to make you understand what I've been saying all this while.'

'No, it took a fight with Amyra.'

'Let's celebrate with a coffee then. What do you think?'

'Is there a special occasion?' Sia could sense some naughtiness in his plan.

'You've finally understood my value. Doesn't that call for a celebration? Come on, let's go.' Ritvik pulled her away.

You cannot hide your emotions from girls; they always sense what's on your mind. Sia had a feeling that Ritvik was taking their relationship to the next level but she kept her suspicions to herself. As he drove towards the nearest Starbucks, Sia couldn't stop herself from glancing at him every few seconds. She didn't want to take the initiative, although she loved it when he looked at her and smiled.

'Are you comfortable?'

'Yes,' she whispered into his ears. The proximity made him feel good.

They reached the coffee shop and Ritvik felt relaxed to see it was not too crowded. It wasn't that he hadn't been alone with Sia before, but it was one of those days when he felt like he could look into her eyes for hours. Words weren't needed as their feelings were communicated loud and clear.

'Will you have something?' Sia asked him.

'It's my treat. I'll get you a coffee.' Ritvik smiled and after perusing the menu for a good minute, he walked towards the cash counter. He looked really hot in his white sneakers and black outfit. Sia found herself observing him closely. Never before had she looked at him with such intentions, and now that she had, she couldn't take her eyes off him. The way his face looked under the lights of the coffee shop made her swoon. This time, when he looked at her, she didn't break eye contact and stared until he let out a shy smile.

Ritvik brought their coffee and, crossing his legs, asked, 'What is it? You look different today.'

'You look different too.'

'I do?'

'You look good in black.'

'You're very observant today. I feel like I am dreaming.' Ritvik tore open a sugar packet.

'Shut up.' Sia threw a sugar packet at him. Little did she know that Ritvik had some serious plans in mind to take a step forward, a step on the road towards a relationship. This is why he had brought her to Starbucks when it was less crowded. It took a while for his nervousness to pass. There was a surprise hidden in her coffee mug and another waited for when she finished her drink.

Every night Ritvik wanted to say 'I love you' to her but managed to restrict it to a 'goodnight'. When it came down to it, she was the only one he wanted, she was the only one he could imagine himself with, she was the only one he thought about when he heard a love song. She was the very last thought running through his mind before he drifted off to sleep. There he was sitting with her, a little nervous and afraid of rejection. It would mean the end of their friendship as he would never be able to look at her the same way. He was ready to take a risk as this was the only way he could take their relationship forward. With each sip of coffee she drank, his heart skipped a beat.

'Why are you looking at my cup so carefully?' Sia asked, confused.

'What? Just enjoy the drink.'

Sia smiled and continued drinking. With the last few sips remaining, Ritvik started freaking out. He had never ever asked anyone out before. The last time he'd loved a girl, she'd started dating someone before he could even express his feelings to her. But with Sia not even aware of what was coming her way, Ritvik was trying hard to stay composed and not panic.

'Are you okay?'

'Only the next few minutes will tell.' Ritvik gripped the couch as tightly as possible when the moment arrived. Sia took the last sip and saw something written at the bottom of the mug with a marker. She looked at it with surprise. She had tears in her eyes when she read aloud what was written. 'Will you be mine?'

When Sia looked up at him, she realized Ritvik was on his knees beside her with a rose in his hand.

'Sorry, I couldn't afford a ring.' He pulled his ear with a sheepish grin on his face.

Sia was smiling and crying at the same time. She had never expected anyone to be interested in dating her. Moreover, she hadn't ever dreamt of being proposed to like this.

'I love you, Sia. My mother once said that it's not a real proposal unless someone gets down on one knee. Will you be my girlfriend?'

Sia was about to speak, when it was time for the second surprise. Ritvik had told the waiter to play his favourite song and make an announcement.

'Sia, Starbucks takes pleasure in disclosing that Ritvik loves you a lot. We request you to accept his proposal and be his soulmate.'

Sia was speechless and, before his knees started hurting, she took Ritvik by his shoulders and made him sit beside her, accepting the rose from him. For the next few seconds, they simply stared at each other. Those few seconds seemed like years to him, and with every moment that passed in silence, he wished for things to go his way. Sia finally reacted.

'Before you start dating me, you need to understand that I'm damaged. I get triggered easily. I have struggled with things. There are nights when I'm curled up like a ball on the floor and I don't talk to anyone. I'll shut you out too. I'm not going to be able to trust you for a while because everyone has always chosen someone else over me. I will need reassurance, I will need you to text me to say that you care when I start to feel bad again. So if you think I'm always happy, that I'll always be positive and smile, you should know the reality. Enter my life only if you can handle it. Also, don't dare touch my heart if you aren't ready for it. I can't lose a friend after a heartbreak. Your friendship means a lot to me and, though I have also started liking you, I can set my desires aside. I love you too, Ritvik, but I am not someone you can flaunt in front of your friends. One thing is for sure though, you will always be proud to have me in your life.'

Without wasting time, Ritvik held her hands and tightened his grip.

'Please understand that I don't want a clichéd relationship. I know that we will have our arguments and problems. I don't want someone to flatter me every second. I want someone who will put me in my place when I'm wrong. I want you to know that I'm willing to stand by your side when you are struggling. I want to be stronger with you. Please be mine.'

'You know what, Ritvik? There are people I wish I hadn't shared my secrets with, and what's funny is that I always thought of you as one of those people. But now I don't regret anything. I really love you.'

Ritvik wiped away her tears and assured her that he would always be there for her no matter what. He would always make her smile even if he was having an off day. They hugged, the embrace taking their happiness to a whole new level. Love isn't just what goes on between the sheets, it's when you accept the person for the way he or she is. Ritvik knew that Sia was not a bombshell, but he loved her for who she was, someone who would never leave just because her expectations weren't met. She had a pure soul and valued relationships because of what she had gone through in the past. He loved her wholeheartedly, and Sia's belief that no one would love her was quashed as they found eternity in each other's arms!

In a world that believes in seven incarnations for lovers, Ritvik accepted Sia for all of time to come. We meet a sea of people but only a few touch our hearts—Ritvik was the one for Sia. Now that Sia had finally found someone who loved her, she didn't want to look back ten years later and think, *We could have been awesome, but I was afraid.* She wanted to give it a try.

Once home, they spent hours talking to each other on the phone before moving to text messages. They shared everything with each other that evening. Ritvik sent her a message first.

I still feel that you should convince your parents and study fashion designing after junior college. There are distance-learning courses available too.

It's not as easy as you think. My dad will disown me if I pursue a career in fashion. According to him, I am not the right kind of girl to do such things. Also, it doesn't suit my family.

There is a solution to everything but we need to sort it out. Don't worry. Muah!

Blush

I love you so much. I can never be the same again, now that I know you. You are my baby.

You have my word that I have never felt anything like this before and I am delighted that you are my boyfriend. I know I will never love anybody the way I love you. You will never regret loving me.

Before you sleep, let me tell you that yes, you are someone I can flaunt. So never think I'll be ashamed of this relationship.

Sia felt as if she was dreaming. No one had ever felt proud to be in her company, but now there was this guy who was boasting about being with her. She was very happy but, at the same time, she was concerned about her best friend, Apurv. She had a sudden urge to tell him that she was dating Ritvik but was scared of what he might say. That summed up the change in their relationship. Nevertheless, she picked up the phone and dialled his number. As expected, it was busy. After trying for more than half an hour, she sent him a message.

I am in a relationship with Ritvik. He asked me out and I accepted. I just wanted to inform you because I don't want to hide anything from you. I tried calling you many times, but you seem to be busy. I'll see you tomorrow in the first half if you are coming to college. I am going out with Ritvik in the second half.

Apurv was on the phone with Amyra when Sia called. But as soon as he read her message, he disconnected. He read the message again and called Sia.

'What? Are you serious or are you drunk again? You and Ritvik? When did this happen?'

'Will you let me speak? Yes, it's true. He proposed to me today at Starbucks. I accepted. So we are officially dating now.'

'But why Ritvik?'

'What kind of a question is that? I love him.'

'No, he is not the right person for you. A girl like you shouldn't be with a guy like him.'

'What do you mean "a girl like me"? And who are you to stop me? Yes, we are good friends but did you ask me before kissing Amyra? No, right? So please don't enforce your opinions on me. Did I tell you whom to date and whom not to?'

Apurv had no answer. He realized that he shouldn't try to control her life.

'I am happy for both of you. I hope you always stay together. So where are you going on your first date?'

'His home.'

'What the fuck? His home on the first date? Are you insane? I hope you understand his intentions. He is just using you.'

'Stop assuming things, Apurv. We are just going to play board games, watch a movie and chill. Don't let your mind run away.'

'You are acting like a fool. He just needs one thing from you and that's why he has called you home. A decent guy will never call a girl home on the first date. Trust me, I know how guys' minds work.'

'Of course. That's why you took Amyra home that night. You think everyone is like you. That's your problem.'

'Is this relationship a way to get back at me for what I did that night?'

'Wow. Did you really say that? I am mature enough to take decisions that are not influenced by others. I love Ritvik and that's why we are together. You're fooling yourself into thinking you are that important.'

Apurv disconnected the call but Sia's mind didn't stop churning. She thought about what Apurv had said, about Ritvik calling her home on the first date, about using her. What if it was true? But she had told him that she was not ready and he had understood. What if Ritvik tore her heart apart? There were many who had used her emotionally, now she was scared of being used physically too.

Please Don't Troll My Heart

'Should I order something to eat?' Ritvik asked Sia, passing her a menu as she sat on the sofa in his living room.

Sia was silent for a moment, her heart pounding. She was nervous because she had never been alone with a guy at his house before. She kept thinking about what Apurv had said. She did trust Ritvik but the baggage of her past terrified her. She was hoping that Ritvik would prove her fears wrong. She buried her face in her hands.

'What's wrong, Sia? Are you okay?'

'Of course I am. Why wouldn't I be?'

Ritvik smiled at her. 'Are you sure? Come on, you can tell me.'

She hesitated at first. She wasn't sure if she should tell him.

'I don't know why but it feels like I can really trust you.'

'Of course you can.' Unexpectedly he put his arms around her. 'Are you crying?'

'No, why would I?'

Ritvik had told her earlier that day that he had made a drawing of her and that it was better than the previous one.

'Where's the drawing?'

'The what?' Ritvik tried to play with her but he couldn't keep it up for long. He reached into his pocket and took out his wallet. Sia looked confused but he had neatly folded the paper.

'Give it to me right now.' Sia was excited to look at her sketch. When she unfolded the paper, the beauty of the girl amazed her. She never thought she could look so beautiful.

'Cute and chubby,' he exclaimed, holding her hand.

Ritvik told her that he had second thoughts about showing it to her because he feared that it would bring back bad memories. But Sia hugged him and planted a small peck on his cheek instead.

'I love you.' The whole time they sat on the sofa, Ritvik stared at her while holding her hand.

'I love you too.' Sia's heart was pounding.

After a pause, Sia spoke again. 'Do you want me to join a gym?'

'No, there's no need for that. You can exercise occasionally to stay fit, but don't lose weight for me. I have no problem because I love you the way you are. You may not have an amazing figure or a flat stomach, but I love you and I don't want you to change.' Ritvik wrapped his hands around her waist.

'I just . . .'

'Shh . . .'

Ritvik took her inside and made her sit on the bed. Sia feared her nightmare was coming true as he sat beside her.

'You can relax.' He gave her a pillow. She rested on it, waiting to see what would happen next. Ritvik lay down beside her and gazed into her eyes. There was hardly space for air to pass between them as they faced each other. Ritvik held her close and lay her head on his chest.

'You don't need a pillow.' He kissed her forehead.

Sia fell asleep like that. Ritvik spent the entire time looking at her, kissing her cheeks. She had replenished his heart with joy. When she got up after a couple of hours, she realized that he had ordered a pizza. The scary thing about a relationship is that you either love that person forever or lose him/her forever. Sia knew that she was going to love Ritvik forever because Ritvik didn't make a move on her even once in all the time that they were together. They talked, watched a movie, played Scrabble and made fun of each other. Her fear lost the battle to love! With every moment, he only made her feel more confident about their relationship and herself. With him, Sia felt safe.

There are two doors—the first leads to an amazing life, and the second one keeps you from getting to the first door. Where Sia had opened the first door, Apurv was still struggling to get past the second. Sia had found a soulmate in Ritvik who understood her emotions, while Apurv was hoping for Amyra to understand his. Though he knew that she wouldn't hurt him, he was still slightly nervous to declare his love for her. After mustering the courage, he was ready to give it a go. He planned to propose to her at the college play rehearsal but, unfortunately, Amyra didn't turn up.

Sorry, Apurv. Something personal has come up and my mom is not allowing me to come to college. I don't know when I'll see you next.

Apurv was dejected because he had been ready to bare his heart to her. He could wait till the next time but it had taken a lot of effort to convince himself to go for it. He felt that day would be perfect to ask her out. After all, it is never easy to express your feelings. Apurv thought of another way and the moment the rehearsals were wrapped up, he went to a vacant classroom. He made sure that he locked it from the inside before texting Amyra.

Hey. Just checked your message. No problem. But can you come online on Instagram for a few minutes? I have to show you something.

Amyra came online.

I am here. What did you want to show me?

The only thing Apurv could feel when he read her message was nervousness. He wanted to give it his best but he also wanted the moment to be over soon. Taking a deep breath, he messaged her.

I am going live. Keep watching!

Will I be able to do it? Will I give it my best or make a fool of myself? I hope the network doesn't betray me. The countdown sent shivers down his spine, but in those few seconds he prepared himself.

3 . . . 2 . . . 1 . . . You are live now.

Once he saw the words on the screen, he started speaking.

'Amyra, this is for you. I want to tell you what is in my heart, no fake sentiments here. We both know we have a very special relationship. Without ever needing to say so, we know how deeply in love we are. But now I want to tell you openly that I love you. When I say "I love you", I don't mean I love you more than you do, I mean I love you more than the bad days ahead of us, more than any fights we may have and more than any obstacles between us. I love you the most. I don't know if you feel the same way about me, but I hope you do. I know together we will live the best years of our lives. Amyra, I love you.'

Apurv ended the live video and called Amyra. She didn't pick up the call and that scared him. He called once more but there was still no response. He left her a message on WhatsApp.

Are you there? Did you see the live video?

Amyra read the message but didn't reply for the next few minutes. She was shocked. She had not expected this from Apurv. She considered him to be a good friend and nothing more.

Why did you do that, Apurv? We were doing well as friends. We even made love to each other. Why did you complicate things by asking for a relationship? Why was a commitment so necessary? I love you, I love you a lot, but only as a friend. I love your company and I don't want to hurt you. What the fuck do I do if to keep myself happy, I have to hurt you? I can't afford to lose your friendship. I wish you understood that.

When you believe someone is really in love with you, it is hard to reject them, especially if they happen to be your friend. You don't know how to convey your feelings without hurting them. She knew that Apurv would be hurt but that was the best way. She finally replied to his proposal via WhatsApp because she couldn't bear the thought of speaking to him on the phone.

I don't know how you will take this, but let me be upfront for the sake of our friendship. Don't get upset. Why can't we just remember the fun times without wanting more? You are everything a girl could want in a boy. The way you confessed your love, I am sure any girl would fall for it. But how do I tell you this? You were kind, you were thoughtful, and you were patient. You took me out on dates and let me get anything I wanted. You made sure

I didn't go to bed without a goodnight text.
However, no matter how good a guy you are,
I just cannot seem to reciprocate those feelings.
You are my best friend and will always be.
Please don't spoil it.

Apurv almost collapsed after reading her text. He felt as if his soul had died. He immediately called her back. As soon as Amyra picked up, he pounced on her. 'Amyra, I love you. You're kidding, right? We even made love to each other. Wasn't that enough? Stop joking. I know you love me. You are just trying to test me but I am not going to fall for it. Please say you love me too.'

'No, Apurv. Please understand. Don't make it harder. I know I am hurting you. I agree that night was memorable but it's not reason enough to commit. I don't feel that connection. It's just that you are special and I feel safe with you. I can be myself around you. Don't overreact please. Do you want me to stop talking to you? I think that would make me sad as I enjoy spending time with you. You are my best friend. Please let's not complicate things.'

Amyra hung up. No one saw her tears. Apurv was shattered and switched off his phone. He felt like the walls were closing in. He had always thought that they were made for each other. Life isn't a game but it still managed to play with him. For hours, he envisioned the hell his life had become. Damn, men cry too! Later that night, when he switched on his phone, there was a message from Amyra.

My heart broke seeing yours break because of me. I know that you have done everything, gone beyond the extra mile. There are so many good things about you that it's almost hard to say no. However, I've thought about this. If you want unconditional love from me, it is not something I can give you. I can't be in a relationship if my gut tells me not to. I know you want to take care of me and love me, but I feel so wrong taking your love and not giving it back. I know you know how I feel and I wish you would see that I can't change. I just want to stop all this and be friends with you like before. Can we? I am sorry but there are certain lines I can't cross.

Apurv replied with a heavy heart. He had no option.

I am sorry for crossing the line. You'll never regret being friends with me.

He kept his phone aside and thought of how they had ended up like this. When did things change and turn into empty conversations? Everything he had built came crashing down in a matter of seconds. He thought of messaging Sia, even typed out a message, but deleted it. He was proved wrong on both occasions. Ritvik, who he thought would be the wrong choice for Sia, turned out to be the perfect partner for her. Amyra, who he thought would be the perfect partner for him, turned out to be the wrong choice. Where Ritvik and Sia's relationship accelerated, Apurv and Amyra were an unfinished poem. They could have been the sweetest story ever written but, like an unfinished poem, they weren't meant to be.

Error 404: Feelings Not Found

How do you un-love someone?
How do you forget the way they walked,
laughed and cried?
How do you turn off the ache in your heart at
the memory of them?
How do you walk away knowing that they
never felt anything for you?

Do you perform a ritual of pretence daily?
Do you cry at the beauty you've lost?
Do you call yourself a fool?
Do you look in the mirror and ask why?

Why did you not love me?
Why did you not see me?

Why did you just want to be friends?
Why does it hurt still?

Apurv was penning poems in his diary when he was supposed to be writing the dialogues for the play. A part of him felt that Amyra wasn't being practical. He thought she was a little scared, which he understood because he was scared too. But he was willing to give it a shot. All that he had got out of this was the impression that he was an okay enough person for people to be friends with but not good enough for a relationship. With each passing minute, he felt more depressed and worthless. He hated that the monster in his head was winning the battle. The fact was that he was yet to see the light at the end of this friendship tunnel.

Ritvik spotted Apurv sitting alone on a bench, writing in his diary. It had been a long time since they had a proper chat. Ritvik sat beside him. 'Are you working on the dialogues for the play?'

'I am sorry, Ritvik. I misunderstood you.'

'What do you mean?'

'I thought Sia would have told you. When she told me about your relationship, I was annoyed as I thought you were using her. But I am happy now. At least the two of you seem happy together.'

Ritvik thought Apurv sounded strange. 'Is everything all right between Amyra and you?'

Apurv turned towards him with sad eyes and told him how he had been friend-zoned. Ritvik couldn't believe what he was hearing, but one look at Apurv bared the truth.

'You are good enough. The person you love just isn't smart enough to realize that,' Ritvik said, trying to make him feel better.

Ritvik even asked Apurv to sort out the differences that had crept in between Sia and him. Though both Apurv and Sia talked to each other and spent time together in college, the chemistry and warmth between them was missing. Their egos prevented them from coming close again. Ritvik assured Apurv that he would try to help resolve things and left when he got a text from Sia. When he told her about Apurv and Amyra, she was furious. She wanted to punch Amyra but Ritvik calmed her down. However, she couldn't keep her cool for long and sent Amyra a text.

I knew a bitch like you can only hurt people. You proved me right and now you shouldn't feel ashamed if someone calls you a slut. If you had no intention of committing to him, why did you sleep with him? You simply betrayed him after satisfying your needs. That's what you did with Ishaan and Pihu too. I'm sure you did something horrible to them. You can never be loyal to anyone. First Ishaan and Pihu, and now Apurv and me. Fuck off, you bitch. A guy like Apurv doesn't deserve you, he deserves better. And don't you worry about him getting hurt, I am there for him, I was always there. You just mind your own business. I'll make sure he's okay.

The message didn't go down well with Amyra.

Fuck off.

She didn't stop there and went on to forward Sia's message to Apurv.

Read what your best friend has written to me. Can't you keep the personal between us? Are you still a schoolkid who goes cribbing to everyone or do you just love getting sympathy from others? I thought we were going to stay friends, and the only thing I wanted was to not complicate our relationship by giving it a title. It hasn't even been a day and you have already made sure the news goes viral. Soon Ritvik will know and then the entire class. They'll even know about the night we spent together.

Apurv, who had no clue about what was going on, was stunned to receive such a nasty message from Amyra after he had politely agreed to be friends. Now he was angry and confused.

> *What's my fault in this? I didn't go and publicize it. I never told anyone about our night. It's you who revealed it to Sia. If you feel that Sia and Ritvik will spread gossip among our classmates, don't worry. I will take care of it. But I request you to stop blaming me for each and every thing that happens. My feelings for you won't change in the span of a few days but I have no expectations now. Yes, I felt bad but, for me, your friendship means much more. I'm sorry for Sia's harsh words. I'll look into it.*

Apurv had hoped that Amyra would change her mind in the future, which is why he had agreed to be friends and act as if nothing had happened.

Why always me? he thought. *Why are things so bad for me all the time? When happiness passes through me, sadness captures it. When the sun shines on me, darkness engulfs it. When everything seems to be all right, something goes against it.*

Apurv was angry with Sia for being so mean to Amyra. But it really wasn't her fault. She did it because she cared for him. Their relationship was already going through a rough phase. While he should have thanked her for expressing the emotions he couldn't, he was boiling with anger at her for doing so. But should he really blame her for the mess and screw things up further? Should he try to resolve their fight, which would make him feel better? Either way, a lump of coal had been tossed into the fire before it even stood a chance of becoming a diamond; all it needed was time.

Apurv ran to the classroom where Ritvik and Sia sat alone. They looked at him in surprise but greeted him with a smile. However, Apurv kept staring at Sia as if she had committed a sin. This scared her because she had never seen Apurv like that before.

Still, faking a smile, she asked, 'Do you have a problem? You look upset. Ritvik told me about you and Amyra. I wish she had proved me wrong.'

Apurv interrupted her. 'Will you cut that crap, now at least?'

Ritvik stood up, anticipating a fight, but before he could say anything, Apurv requested him to leave as he wanted to talk to Sia alone. Sia was scared but, looking at the intensity of the situation, she requested Ritvik to step out. As he left, Ritvik wondered if they would be able to resolve the conflict.

'I want to talk to you,' said Apurv. 'Who gave you the permission to message Amyra on my behalf? Did I ask you to be my lawyer? You just do what you want and at the end of the day I have to suffer because of you. Why should I? You are enjoying your life with Ritvik but you have a problem with everything I do. When I kissed her, you interrupted us and started screaming as if we had done something wrong. You had a problem when we spent time at home. But you are okay with going to Ritvik's house. What is your problem? Why don't you just fuck off?'

Sia was surprised at Apurv's attack. 'Why are you talking to me like this? I just didn't like the way she rejected you. I was just supporting you. I don't have any problems apart from the words you are using.'

'Yes, she rejected me. But does that give you the right to speak to her like that? I had no problem with her decision. It was totally her wish, and I accepted it. We were okay with being just friends but you had a problem with that too. You are ruining my life because of your issues with her. Do I interfere in every small thing you do with Ritvik? Please don't butt into my personal life.' Apurv had never been this furious before.

'Fine, let's end it then.'

'End what?'

'Our friendship. What's the use of being friends if we can't share our feelings with each other? Why should we even talk to each other? Let's end it. Delete my number from your phone. I don't need you.' Sia's heart ached as she said this but no one could see it, not even Apurv. 'You think I will cry if you do this

145

emotional drama. I don't need this in my life. I don't need anyone. Not even you. Buzz off.'

Apurv walked towards the door and before leaving, he turned towards her. 'Yes, let's end it. Once and for all. Don't try to contact me ever again.'

Sia and Apurv had ended their friendship but if that was what they both wanted, why did the memories still hurt so much? As Tim Burton said, 'Every story has a beginning, a middle, and an end.' And although they had called it an end, something was missing in the middle. They were both unsure of whether their story was over or not and secretly hoped that the other didn't close the book so soon.

The words we speak in anger often destroy relationships, forcing us to drift apart from the people that mean so much to us. What do you do when the one who broke your heart is the only one who can fix it? Apurv was devastated as he had lost not only Sia but also Amyra. Sia, at least, had Ritvik to help her through this tough time. In the midst of all this, everyone overlooked how Amyra felt because she never spoke to anyone about her anguish. She would have been much happier had she erased her past. But it was still there, tearing her apart. No, it wasn't because of her past that she had denied herself a relationship with Apurv, but the denial took her back to her schooldays when friendships were broken in a similar manner.

Pihu, Ishaan and Amyra had parted ways because of one unintentional action that Amyra had taken. Just as Sia had interfered between Apurv and Amyra, Pihu too insisted on having a say in Amyra's relationship with Ishaan. This affected the bond between them. However, none of them had wrong intentions.

The past was repeating itself once again, although the tables had now been turned. Sia was now in the same situation as Amyra had been when Ishaan chose friendship over a relationship. Amyra had not got a chance to prove herself, and Sia wasn't getting one now. In the war of emotions, Apurv had hurt Sia and Amyra could feel her pain. After shifting schools, she even tried contacting Ishaan and Pihu but all her attempts failed. Even after two years, she wished to meet them and explain her actions and apologize.

Wasn't it ironic? She had told Apurv to stay strong but she couldn't do so herself? Did she still love Ishaan? Is that why she had friend-zoned Apurv? Or was her subconscious mind hiding some secrets? Whatever it was, the house of cards, with a misplaced whisper, was tumbling.

Ego-1, Friendship-0

The clock kept moving but their lives didn't. One step in the wrong direction and they stood still. Ritvik was the mediator between Sia and Apurv as they stopped communicating. Both of them couldn't sleep at night because of their troubled minds. Apurv wanted to hang out with Amyra but he felt like the boundaries had been marked. Ritvik too had realized that they needed to find a solution because Sia always looked dejected. The inter-college festival was inching closer. Rehearsals were in full swing and that was the only time that all four of them came under one roof. It was on one such day that Ritvik called Apurv to meet him face-to-face. He wanted to know what was running through his mind, the way he approached life and relationships.

'What are you seeking from Amyra? Why don't you just call it off?' Ritvik asked Apurv as they ate a sandwich in the canteen.

'I can't. Can you just end your relationship with Sia? Would you have given up if she had said no to this relationship?' Apurv tried to make Ritvik understand that it was not easy to move on even though he had no hope.

'At least I wouldn't have faked a relationship.'

'I know your concern, Ritvik, but it's not as clear as it seems. She is hiding something. How should I explain this? She is going through something, that's all I can figure out.'

'It's your perception, all rubbish. She is just playing with your emotions and you're allowing her to. Sia wasn't wrong, and I am saying this after a month.' Ritvik raised his tone this time.

Apurv was shocked when he realized that it had actually been a month.

'Has she spoken to her parents about fashion designing? You said she was going to this week. The HSC board exams are approaching. She shouldn't put it off any further.' Apurv showed concern for Sia but didn't look at Ritvik. Whenever he asked about Sia, he avoided eye contact.

'Wow, brother, I don't understand you guys. She keeps asking me if you have started preparing for the engineering entrance exam and you keep asking me about her fashion designing. Why don't you both simply put your egos aside and talk to each other? Am I a postman?' Ritvik shook his head thinking how impossible his two friends were to deal with.

'No, I don't want to talk to her. She wanted to end the friendship and I accepted her decision. If she wants to talk to me, she can do so.'

They got up as it was time for rehearsal. As they walked out, Ritvik said, 'Please mark my words about Amyra. It's high time now.' He was sure that Apurv still cared about Sia. However, he knew that Apurv wouldn't initiate a conversation. He thought of requesting Sia to do so. He was ready to do all that was needed but neither of them was ready to pull back.

Ritvik was waiting for the right time to bring up the topic but he hardly got a chance during the rehearsals because Apurv was with Amyra all the time and Sia was not in a state to open up. But as soon as the rehearsals ended and they reached the nearby mall, he decided to ask her indirectly. 'Did you talk to your parents?'

'I did, but they are still quite adamant. I need to prove myself to them somehow.'

'I have already taken care of it. At the next rehearsal, the seniors will talk to you about it. You will be in charge of the costume designs for the play along with a few delegates to help you out. You also need to create an Instagram account. You can't do the tailoring work but at least you have ideas that you can share.'

Sia was taken aback and kissed him then and there. 'I am so lucky to have you.'

Ritvik put his arms around her and tightened his grip to show his affection. Sia loved his scent but before she could say anything, he handed her a piece of paper.

'Apurv gave this to me today. He wrote something for you when I told him that you were going to try convincing your parents. Please read it.'

'Why the fuck did you have to spoil my mood? Aren't you happy that all my time is for you? Apurv blamed me for the chaos in his life and you still want me to talk to him.' Sia exploded without reading what was written on the paper.

'Please just read it.'

You are the edge of the water rolling up to the beach
You know the struggle of the sand
Your desires you may never reach,
Yet you continue to conquer the lands.
But I tell you now,
Enjoy the climb, the feel and the fall
Because secretly,
You are the entire sea,
and within you, you have it all.

Sia was overwhelmed as she read the poem, but she didn't show it. Instead, she tore the paper and threw it into the trash. She was angry, not because Ritvik was taking sides, but because Apurv couldn't come up and speak to her directly.

'It's because of him that our relationship is at this stage. He had no place in my life the day he blamed me. I just don't want to talk about him.'

'Why don't you accept that you still care about him? If his absence didn't bother you, you wouldn't have dumped his poem in the trash. Relationships don't function like this. Why don't you just go and talk to him?'

'Is it so difficult to understand that I have moved on?'

'No, that's where the problem lies. You haven't moved on. Also, it was your idea to end everything, right? Now can't you just go back and tell him you were wrong? You shouldn't have said that.'

'That's great. If he really was my friend, he would have stayed away from Amyra. Look at what he got in return. Just because I asked him to end it, he didn't have to. I don't want him back unless he talks straight to my face.'

Ritvik couldn't understand why people were so complicated. Both Sia and Apurv were adamant and ready to end the relationship but they couldn't put aside their egos.

It was one of those nights when Apurv was lying on his bed, looking at the ceiling, letting his feelings run through his mind. The overwhelming emptiness reminded him of his loneliness. Despite being surrounded by everyone in college, he had no one to share his feelings with. Amyra was the one he talked to more often than anyone but he never shared how hurt he was because of her rejection. They went out for coffee, drinks, movies and long drives, but there was something missing in their relationship—the acceptance. That night, however, Apurv couldn't suppress his feelings. He messaged her.

I have never been mad at you. All that mattered to me was seeing you smile. We could talk about anything, from the most random topics to serious conversations. We did everything that a couple generally does, without calling it a relationship. I felt like we were close enough for me to ask you out on dates and try to work towards calling you mine. But every time the answer was no. Why don't I deserve a chance? What is the worst that could happen? You waste a little bit of time? But you could be missing out on the best thing that might ever happen to you, because that's what meeting you was for me.

Amyra was quick to reply as she was watching a movie on her phone. The message didn't irritate her but the way Apurv would open a closed chapter every now and then, hoping for a better climax, brought a smile to her face.

> *Apurv, you are a sweetheart. Throw away these negative thoughts. Of course, you are the best thing that has ever happened to me, but I don't want to waste even a little bit of time. Don't try to label it, let us just be the way we are. *Kisses* for your cuteness. See you tomorrow in college.*

With no clarity, his heart was slowly losing all hope. Emotionally, he was fragile. In his search for love, he had lost even his closest and most trustworthy friend.

The next day, when he reached the campus, he saw Sia and Ritvik walking in his direction. Ritvik waved to greet him but Sia purposely looked down at her phone, pretending to text someone. Amyra was also in the same corridor, and every time she saw Apurv and Sia pass each other without talking, she felt guilty. She wanted to talk to Sia but she knew she wouldn't take it well. Ritvik saw that pain in her eyes and decided to speak with her, hoping that she would sort things out.

Later, after exchanging texts, they met in the library where no one could see them.

'Are you aware of the things going on between Sia and Apurv?' Ritvik whispered, pretending to read his notes.

'I know and I feel guilty. I wouldn't have shared the message with him if I knew it would end their friendship. But what can I do? I am helpless.'

'Do you love someone else? Are you in a relationship with someone else?' Ritvik asked, trying to find out the reason behind her not accepting Apurv's proposal.

'No, I am not. If you want to know the truth, let me tell it to you. I like Apurv, maybe even love him. Yes, I do. Just because I don't admit it doesn't mean I have no feelings for him. But I just don't want to be in a relationship and hurt him later.'

'What the fuck? You love him? Are you fucking serious?' Ritvik was shocked because the sole reason behind this mess was Amyra friend-zoning Apurv and here she was confessing her love for him. Ritvik was outraged by what she was saying but, since they were in the library, he was forced to keep his voice down.

'Yes, I do. But I don't want a relationship. I trust you because you came here to sort things out between all of us. I hope that by revealing these things, you won't mess it up further.'

Ritvik got up and left as he couldn't understand why Amyra would not accept her love for Apurv. If they were meant to be, what was stopping her? It couldn't be Apurv's friendship with Sia because she was equally hurt by that ending. Or was it really because of the insecurity that comes with every relationship? Ultimately, nothing went Ritvik's way although he tried his best.

Inside she's a wreck,
When you see her she looks perfectly fine
Deep down her mind is a mess,
When she's with you she looks happy
But she's alone; fragile,
The girl with broken dreams; defeated by destiny
She wants to escape from the people around,
To a city unknown
And perhaps one day,
When you ask her 'Are you okay?'
For once, she'll say, 'I'm fine.'
And it wouldn't
Be a lie.

It's Not Funny Any More

Two months later:

I keep writing these poems,
emptying my heart out on paper,
thinking somehow
this will make it feel less hollow,
thinking someday
these words won't be so tortured,
but every scratch of my pen,
every patch of black or blue
confessing something that just
didn't fit right
looks so vacant,
and everything I say
is starting to sound the same.

I am pulling words from a thesaurus,
trying to rephrase the ache into something
I haven't felt before these past few months,
trying to justify
why I haven't been able to fix this yet
talking myself into a frenzy
this ink is gasoline
and combustion
is something with which I am all too familiar!

Gasping, Apurv wiped the sweat off his forehead with his sleeve as he submitted the voice-over poem to the seniors for the play. In the past two months, Sia had drifted away from him while he had become immune to the pain he felt every time he was with Amyra. Ritvik didn't disclose anything, keeping his word to Amyra, but her absurd behaviour these past few weeks disturbed everyone. It was not that she was arrogant or giving people attitude, but she wasn't able to recollect things that she earlier had at her fingertips, giving the impression that she was doing it on purpose. She had forgotten about the class before and had once mentioned forgetting her way back home, but in the past couple of weeks things had become very strange.

'Amyra, what's wrong with you. You are repeatedly forgetting the lines,' the seniors yelled at her.

'I don't know. I am trying my best.' Amyra was almost sobbing.

'You have stopped concentrating. Earlier you would forget a few lines, but now you are unable to remember entire scenes. Tomorrow, you won't remember your role. This will not work. We don't have much time now.'

'It's okay, don't worry,' Apurv interrupted as he saw the sadness in her eyes. 'Do you want me to change your lines to something easier?'

'No, it's fine. I'll manage.'

No one understood what was wrong with Amyra, but Apurv sensed it was something terrible. She not only forgot her dialogues, but also her classes on a regular basis, and once her chemistry test. The next day, she actually forgot her role in the play. Apurv tried to help her remember but her memory was foggy. Apurv asked for some time alone with her and took her to the college canteen where they ordered a coffee and sat at a table away from everyone. There were not a lot of students because it was a weekend.

'Here's your coffee.' Apurv gave her a wide smile, pulling her cheeks to make her feel better.

'Thanks.' She faked a smile.

'Are you lost somewhere, or are there some issues at home? Why are you not able to concentrate? I mean, you knew the lines and had rehearsed them so many times. How could you not remember? How could you forget simple dialogues or your chemistry test for that matter?' Apurv held her hand and tried to comfort her.

'I just feel like being alone. Leaving everything behind. This is not the place I should be. That's what I am told.' Amyra avoided Apurv's eyes.

'What are you talking about?'

'I don't feel like being with anyone. Can you take me somewhere? I just want to get away from this noise. I just want peace.' Amyra pulled her hand away and took a sip of the coffee.

'Should I take you home? There's no one there. We could watch a movie and chill out,' Apurv suggested.

'Your house? Do you stay nearby?'

Amyra looked confused. This shocked Apurv as she had been to his house before. It was where they had had sex. *Is she pretending or is there something seriously wrong with her? Forgetting classes and tests was fine, forgetting dialogues too is okay, but how could she forget the place where we were intimate for the first time? I have heard that you always remember your first time. Then what is fucking wrong with her?* These thoughts ran through Apurv's mind as he stared at her. Maybe she was playing with him.

'What kind of a question is that? You have been there. You weren't so drunk.' Apurv winked and got up to leave.

'Me? No, I have never been to your place. I don't remember going there.' Amyra looked at him with an innocent face.

'Okay, stop kidding.'

'I'm not. Why would I come to your house?'

Apurv ignored her, passing it off as a silly prank, and left the canteen, pulling her by her hand. While driving home, he couldn't help but worry about her behaviour. He kept stealing glances at her, thinking about what she was going through. Was she emotionally exhausted or completely drained out?

Apurv initially thought she was joking, but when she insisted that she couldn't remember ever coming to his house, it scared him. She had done this far too many times for it to be a prank. The only option he had was to ignore it because there was nothing he could do. The thought of calling or meeting her parents came to his mind, but he knew that Amyra wouldn't like it. He remembered the time when she had forgotten her sister's birthday. In the weeks since she had started behaving absurdly, Apurv had always been there for her. But it upset him. She was the sort of mystery that took a lifetime to solve.

Apurv parked his Vespa and went upstairs, this time much more confident when he passed the watchman. In the elevator, he sighed. 'Thank God, this time that rascal didn't look at us. Remember how he looked at us the last time?'

'You have a good sense of humour. I have never been to this place.'

Sudeep Nagarkar

'Oh! Not again. Stop it.' Apurv opened the elevator door and Amyra looked around as if trying to recollect if she had been there before. Apurv opened the front door to his house. Everything seemed new to Amyra, but she didn't tell him. Apurv got her a glass of water and made her sit on the couch in the living room. After discussing the play for some time, he shifted the topic to her schooldays, thinking that it would bring her comfort.

'You mentioned being close to someone called Pihu. Is she as hot as you? I might as well try flirting with her.'

'I am not in touch with her. After I changed schools, we stopped interacting. It was entirely my fault. I played a prank without realizing how much it could hurt her. I wish I could meet her at least once and apologize.'

'It's okay. Life is about moving on.' Apurv was sitting close to her and eating chips.

'Why are you asking me this? Didn't you know her? In fact, you were her good friend.' Amyra's face was blank.

'I wish!' Apurv winked.

He was a little surprised. *How would I know her school friend? I only met her in college. What is she up to? I am losing it now. Even pranks have certain limits. If I didn't love her, I would scream at her.* Gradually his patience wore thin, but he didn't show it. He pretended to be calm.

164

Sitting so close to Apurv, Amyra couldn't help notice just how muscular his shoulders were and how lush his lips looked. She let her gaze slide over the rest of his body. She had seen him a thousand times, but he seemed so different that day. When she looked into his eyes once again, his expression was intense. For a moment, Amyra thought that maybe he was angry, but before she could think about it further, he covered her mouth in a hungry kiss. She responded immediately, surprising herself. Suddenly, Apurv pushed her away as if he had been burnt.

'I'm sorry, Amyra,' he said in a strangled voice. 'That wasn't right.'

'It's okay,' Amyra said, looking at the floor. She was afraid of seeming too eager or disappointed. In fact, she wasn't quite sure how to react to that kiss. Amyra couldn't help but wonder if Apurv's heart was beating as fast as hers or if he was feeling the same desire as she was. However, a few minutes later both of them gave in to the temptation. Every inch of their bodies was soaked in love. Amyra was lost totally in the heat of the moment. Her touch made him go weak. Amyra blushed and felt prickles of pleasure move up her arms as he grew hard in her hand. She squeezed instinctively, feeling the muscle throb and flex, forcing her to tighten her grip. Finally, he pushed her down on to the bed and climbed on top of her. He kicked off his shoes, quickly got out of his jeans and dragged a blanket over them.

'Open your eyes,' he whispered as he slid into her. She felt very tight.

There was a pause. Every sensation was new and fiercely familiar at the same time, shocking Amyra with recognition and surprise.

'I'm scared to move,' he said, laughing.

'Why, will you lose it?'

He nodded. 'Well, this is fucking great, isn't it?'

'Yes, it is, Ishaan.'

Apurv was surprised to hear Ishaan's name, but her eyes were closed and Apurv didn't want to stop. Though it should have alerted him that something was awfully wrong, he went with the flow. Desire slammed through her, leaving her shaking for more. He gently kissed the tears from her cheeks and held her gaze as he slid inside her again.

'Ah, God!' He quivered, prolonging the moment. Then he began to move again, undone by her fire, torn to shreds by the passion she ripped from him. Her wet heat engulfed him, burnt him and caressed him to the point of insanity. Soon he was thrusting madly, lost inside her, completely unaware of his surroundings. She screamed, her nails digging into his back as she arched one last time before collapsing under him, shuddering convulsively.

'I'm yours! I'm . . .' A groan tore from deep inside her chest as his release surged through him, flinging him briefly into a place full of light and sound before leaving him gasping as he gathered her close, trembling and shaken.

Apurv lay beside her and for a few seconds, they stared at the ceiling, their breath still heavy.

'Ishaan, I so wanted to do this with you! You are amazing, Ishaan.' Amyra breathed out a luxurious sigh.

That was it! Apurv was irritated with Amyra for repeatedly addressing him as Ishaan. Anyone's ego would be hurt in such a situation and Apurv was no god. He looked at her in anger.

'Who the fuck is Ishaan? I am Apurv. Have you lost it? Enough is enough. Just get out of here. Right away. I don't care about anything. I just want you out of this house. Go fuck Ishaan or do whatever you feel. Just get out of my house, my life. I can't handle this any more.'

What the fuck! Was she hallucinating or fantasizing? Was she pretending or losing her memory? Did she think I was Ishaan when she said I was friends with Pihu?

Was this an alarming sign of something horrendous coming their way?

It was another day filled with malice and hate for himself for the things he couldn't change easily. Apurv stayed home that day, contemplating whether he should end it all or carry on in a show of strength.

However, all his thoughts disappeared into thin air the moment Amyra called, asking him to pick her up. It was 11 p.m., but without paying heed to the time and forgetting his rage, he set out on his Vespa to the location she had mentioned.

'Where are you? I have just arrived,' he asked her on the phone. Parking his Vespa on the side stand, he scanned the area.

'I am not exactly sure, but I think I am at the Andheri bus depot.'

Her response confused Apurv because he was at that very location.

'My phone battery is about to die. Let me find a landmark; this lane looks like the McDonald's one near the bus depot.'

'Is this another fucking prank? I've been driving up and down this lane but you are nowhere to be seen. Where are you? Chuck all this; send me your location on WhatsApp.'

'No, let me check.'

Shortly after that, before Apurv could receive her location on WhatsApp, her phone died. After the bizarre phone call, he drove around the area asking people if they had seen her. He even tried calling her a couple of times hoping she had a spare battery. Till 1 a.m., he waited, hoped, searching for her at possible locations. He feared the worst. Just thinking about something bad happening to her gave him goosebumps.

It was odd as he had been right at the spot she had mentioned and had spoken to her moments before, yet she was gone as if she had ceased to exist. Where did she disappear all of a sudden? Did some tragedy strike? Was she safe in the darkness of the city?

And Then She Said It

Amyra was a question with no answer, a song paused midway. Not knowing is what haunts you. It had been forty-eight hours and Amyra's phone was still switched off. She didn't come to college the day after the incident, not even for the rehearsals. Apurv didn't reveal anything to anyone as he was not sure about what had happened. Sia and Ritvik felt she was just on leave but the truth was different. Hours turned into days but there was no means of getting in touch with Amyra.

None of their classmates knew where she was, and with each passing day Sia could see the restlessness in Apurv's eyes. Apurv decided to go to Amyra's house a week later, to the place where he had once dropped her off on her sister's birthday. On the way to her house, he kept thinking about what could have gone wrong. He remembered Sia telling him that Amyra had left her old school suddenly and shifted to another one. Was she a con girl? But what would she get out of it? First school and now college.

Once he reached, he checked the message he had sent her the previous night but it was still undelivered. He read it again before walking towards her apartment.

I want you to know that I loved you. I even loved you when you decided that you didn't love me. I cannot express these emotions in words the same way I cannot describe the way it felt to have you rip it all to pieces. I prayed every five minutes that you would call me and tell me you had made a mistake. Even today, I pray every night and hope to see your name appear on my phone. There's nothing I miss more than you. I've destroyed some of my friendships because you were more important to me. You have shattered my heart, but you have not shattered my love. Love is not something that can be cast aside and broken. I know you feel it too, deep inside, and my love allows me to genuinely hope that you will realize it one day.

Tears rolled down his cheeks on reading the message as only he understood the pain of losing her. He walked inside her apartment building with shaky steps. As he stood in front of her door, he realized that the surname written on it was not hers. He guessed that it might be a rented apartment, but when he rang the bell and asked for Amyra the man's answer made his blood run cold. He couldn't believe what he had heard and stood there frozen in shock.

'There's no one called Amyra here.'

Fuck! How's this even possible? I clearly remember dropping her off at this location. She had entered this very building. Is he fucking lying to me?

'Are you sure? I know she stays here.'

'No, beta, no such girl ever stayed here.'

'Is there anyone in this building by this name? Please tell me if you have any idea.'

The man looked at him for a few seconds before speaking sternly. 'Don't try to act smart. I know you college boys use this trick to find girls' addresses. If you are eyeing my daughter, I will call the police right now. Don't you dare knock on my door again.'

He slammed the door shut on Apurv's face. Apurv was dejected but he didn't give up. He thought the man might be faking it. No one would call for their daughter in front of an unknown guy. He approached the watchman of the building who was reading a newspaper.

'Who are you? How did you enter without writing your name in the register?'

'Uncle, you were lost in reading some interesting news, so I didn't disturb you.' Apurv mocked him before asking, 'Have you seen this girl here before? I had dropped her here once.'

The watchman looked at the photograph keenly and answered after spitting. 'No, never. What has happened?'

'Please try to remember. She stays here. I dropped her here one night.'

'No. She doesn't stay here or else I would have known. My duty is to take care of this building. How will I not know the residents? Also, if you dropped her here at night, I'm not too sure because my shift is usually during the day.'

'Should I ask the night watchman?' Apurv's disappointment was visible.

'It's no use. He is new here. It's hardly been a week since he joined. But, Bhaiya, you just dropped her here. Who knows, she might have been visiting someone. There are a few guys here who stay together and work for some computer company. Such scenes are common at their place. There are so many girls who visit them that it's difficult to keep track.'

Apurv walked away but the conversation with the watchman had disturbed him. Did she really come here to meet someone? Her boyfriend? Apurv even asked all the shopkeepers around about her, but it was of no use. He asked the creeps who he expected would have all the information about the girls in the neighbourhood, but even they had not seen her. Apurv finally had to accept that Amyra had lied to him about where she stayed. He had never asked her to take him to her house. She was the one to visit his house both times. Was that a conscious decision? Apurv was losing all respect for her. He really wanted to believe her but this time she had left him with nothing. Her existence was nothing but a hollow lie. Even after knowing each other, he felt as if they were no better than strangers.

It's painful to know that you are the only one who's in love while the other person hardly cares. Apurv could barely sleep these days; all he did was pen down his thoughts.

> *I got up in the middle of the night. All I could hear was a loud cry coming from someone who was hurt, the cry was familiar to me. I searched for that someone who was crying so loudly. I looked around the room even though it was dark. I tried to calm myself but the voices were so loud that I could really feel the pain. There was no one, until I stood in front of the mirror. I could see my reflection, those tears and the pain.*

He needed someone with whom he could share everything. He ultimately decided to tell Sia what had happened. But his fingers went numb when he tried calling her. It had been ages since they had spoken. Things were not like before. He finally settled on a text.

I am sorry. We cross each other every day, but let's talk tomorrow. Let's not get into the 'We just stopped talking' zone which is the reason so many friendships end.

Sia's response surprised Apurv.

What took you so long to message? Love you.

Apurv broke down as soon as he read the message. She still cared for him. He had misjudged her. They were two different people with different attitudes, but the one thing that held them together was their friendship. Apurv immediately dialled her number.

His heartbeat was louder than the phone ringing. He paced around his room nervously because he was talking to her after such a long time. Her 'hello' gave him goosebumps, but at the same time he felt a soothing calm. He sobbed like a child, loud enough for Sia to hear. They had finally overcome their egos to talk to each other. Sia found it hard to control her tears but to avoid an emotional breakdown, she stopped herself. For the next couple of minutes, no one spoke. But every emotion was expressed—happiness, pain and love. And if someone still believed that friendships weren't special, that person was a fool.

Sia finally broke the silence. 'Just because we don't talk any more doesn't mean that I have forgotten about you. It doesn't mean that I no longer care. The truth is that I still do. I did my best to check up on you, to see how you were doing. But every time I felt the urge to talk to you, I remembered that we were strangers and that you didn't want me in your life.'

'No, you didn't want me in your life, that's why you never tried to contact me. I even sent you a poem through Ritvik. I used to ask him about you every day.'

'You couldn't ask me directly?'

'I felt guilty. But I want you to know that I'm still here. I'll still give you my shoulder to lean on no matter what time it is or what I'm doing. I'll not hesitate because, most of the time, I wish that you were still talking to me. I missed your presence, you being my best friend, I just missed you.'

And they were friends again with just one message. Sometimes we are too hesitant to solve our problems in a simple way.

The following day, while Sia waited with Ritvik for Apurv in the canteen, she had mixed feelings. She was nervous about talking to Apurv in person after such a long time but excited to be reunited with her best friend. A volcano of emotions erupted when he finally entered the canteen. The only thing that was missing was the slow-motion effect like in a movie. All they wanted was a friendship like the one they had. Not a day went by without the two of them wondering why they fell out. Why had their friendship cracked? But one hug was enough to melt their hearts. Isn't it weird how you can go from being everything to nothing because of one misunderstanding? Ritvik was the only one who had tried, but failed, to bring them together. However, friends do find a way to get back if they really want to.

'I am sorry. Please forgive me,' Sia said with tears in her eyes.

Apurv remained quiet but his emotions were visible on his face. They couldn't believe that they were finally sitting in front of each other.

'I don't know why we drifted apart. I want us to be friends again, just like we used to be. I want us to stay up all night talking about what's in our hearts because no one can make me feel as comfortable as you do and no one has my trust the way you still do.'

'I'll be there for you until you find someone better, which I am sure you won't ever,' Sia winked.

Ritvik was probably the happiest person that day after seeing the lost spark in Sia's eyes return. Friendship is about sharing the deepest parts of your soul with someone. Their friendship was still special in each and every sense.

'So, did you guys kiss? I could have gone further, but as we are meeting after a long time, I thought I'd be a bit decent.' Apurv forgot about his worries for a second.

'Will you ever change?' Sia asked.

'No, I am just asking. You can also use the parking space if you want. I can guide you through the steps.'

'Shut up.'

Apurv told them what had happened with Amyra at the bus stop. They were surprised because they had thought that Apurv knew where she was all this time. Sia tried to help him find her but there was little that she could do.

It was one of those days when the stars were in hiding, blanketed by the thick city smog. Apurv sat in a corner of his dimly lit room, thinking about Amyra's smile. The broken lamp, the dying bulb that flickered hopelessly, the torn photographs and the empty glass of beer were all witness to his heartbreak. He kept coming back to the same things every time he spoke to Sia.

'We haven't been doing anything apart from discussing her for the past few days. You should get a life,' Sia said as she tried hanging up on him. His constant cribbing was getting on her nerves.

'It wouldn't have mattered this much if she had continued attending classes regularly. What frustrates me is that none of the shopkeepers near her house recall seeing her.'

The conversation continued and despite repeated attempts by Sia to calm Apurv down, he continued to stress himself out.

His parents were out of town for the weekend and he had locked himself in his room. He played their favourite song till he could take it no longer. Then he turned to what helped him cope with the pain the best. By the end of the night, there was a collection of bottles at the foot of his bed.

As he scrolled through her profile on Facebook, he came across a post that suddenly made sense to him.

Never be dependent on one person because if they fail to be by your side, you will lose all your strength. You'll be buried under the weight of it all, waiting for that one person to pull you up. If they fail to show up, you'll be crushed. Learn to make your scars your strength instead.

After reading her status, he was so overcome with emotions that he proceeded to smash the wind chimes that were tinkling half-heartedly. They were, after all, the ones she had gifted him. He often hoped that destroying the tangible memories associated with her would lessen some of his pain, but the harder he tried, the worse it became.

The next day, Ritvik finally got Amyra's address after forcing a peon to get it for him from the student records. When he told Apurv and Sia what he had done, they were overjoyed.

'How did you do it, bro?' Apurv hugged him in excitement.

'Talent, you see.'

'Fuck off. But you just nailed it.'

'You know, there is one more reason. When you and Sia weren't talking to each other, I met Amyra alone to ask if she could help me resolve the issue. It was then that she told me that she loved you but still couldn't be with you. I found it strange. My curiosity is the only reason I took a risk and bribed the peon. Here is her address.'

'This is so strange,' Apurv said. 'I dropped her off at Andheri and that's where she was when she called me that night. I even asked why we were heading to Andheri when she told me that she lived in Versova. But she denied staying in Versova. And now this address says Versova. Why did she give me a fake address and pretend to enter the apartment in Andheri?' Apurv was very confused.

'I hope the truth isn't something awful,' Sia said.

Each step towards Amyra's Versova address killed him. When they entered the building, they saw her surname on a nameplate. Since the elevator wasn't working they had to climb the stairs to the fifth floor.

'Mine is fourth. Hers is fifth,' Apurv said, panting.

'What?' Sia asked.

'Floors. Mine is fourth and hers is fifth.'

'So?' questioned Ritvik.

'I am just trying to keep calm.'

'Don't worry, she will be at home.' Sia comforted him.

Standing in front of the door, Apurv took a deep breath and looked at both Sia and Ritvik for reassurance. He rang the bell but no one opened the door. He gave it another try and finally a girl appeared. She was younger than them, but she looked like Amyra.

'Amyra?' Apurv asked, feeling confident. He had expected her parents to open the door.

'Didi is not here. She has gone with Mom and Dad. You are Apurv, right?'

Apurv was surprised. 'Yes. How do you know me?'

'I have seen your pictures on Didi's phone.'

'Can we come inside?' Sia asked.

The girl welcomed them in. After offering them water, she revealed that she was Amyra's younger sister Nivi. The house felt silent and haunted. Apurv wanted to know the truth behind Amyra's disappearance. 'Where has Amyra gone?'

'To meet a baba for Ayurvedic medicine. They left a couple of weeks ago and will return only next week. My aunt is staying with me in the meantime, but she's gone to work now.'

'Medicine for what?'

'What happened to her?' Sia asked after Apurv.

'Alzheimer's.'

'What?'

'It's an incurable disease, but medicine can slow its progress. She has an eraser in her mind, according to Mom.'

Both Sia and Apurv were horrified to know that there was something wrong with her medically. Ritvik, too, was dumbfounded. None of them could believe the truth.

'What does that mean?' Apurv stammered.

'It makes her forget things. A mental death will come before the physical. Even surgery can't cure it. Soon, she will forget us. You, Mom, Dad and me. Everyone.'

'What? You are joking, right? She is hiding somewhere inside, I know. Amyra, come out now.' Apurv was convinced that Nivi was playing a sick prank.

'No. I am not lying. Mom told me this. She is dying.'

'Amyra knew about this?' Apurv asked.

'Yes.'

Apurv's world turned dark the moment Nivi uttered those words. Was this for real? Was Amyra dying? The word 'death' weighed heavy in his head. He stood there, hollow and empty. It's said that when a person dies, their memories live on forever. But for Amyra, the memories were dying first. Was this the reason that she had friend-zoned Apurv?

Still, Can She Be Happy?

Pieces thrown everywhere
Pieces of my heart, torn apart by the air
Silence.
Nothing but silence after the offensive blare
I can't take any more of this repulsive snare
My soul fell to my knees feeling weak and
unaware!
A writer, whose connection with pen and
paper would now be rare.

Apurv's world fell apart when he heard about Amyra's illness. His heart was in pieces. He knew she wasn't ready to die. She had so many things left to experience. The shards of his shattered soul contained memories that he wished to remember, but Amyra was forgetting it all. His research on the Internet revealed that it was a rare disease in which the brain decomposed before the body.

'But she is only sixteen!' her mom had said to the doctor. She was told to prepare herself for the inevitable. Neither surgery nor medicine would cure her and soon she would not even be able to use her phone. All memories would fade away. There was no fixed pattern and sometimes she would forget in fragments and recollect it later, but gradually everything would be erased, the most recent memories first. She was advised to quit college but it was her decision to continue because she wanted to spend time with Apurv. No one took her seriously when she first started forgetting about classes and tests. But she had known from the start. This is why she had not accepted Apurv's proposal. Apurv felt so guilty for the way he had treated her the last time they were together.

He tried calling her again, but there was no response. Her parents might have taken her phone away. He couldn't stop himself from dropping a text.

I am sorry that I was rude to you the day you came home. Your love for me is the most precious gift I have ever received. I now know the truth and my life has come to a standstill.

Can't we relive those days again and again? My life before I met you was nothing. I always struggled to find true love and now that I've got it, destiny has played its part. I sometimes think God is taking revenge on me for something I did in my past life. Please come back soon and I promise to fulfil every last wish of yours.

He had so much to say, but his words were like sand being washed away by a tide of emotions. He was determined to fulfil her desire to meet Pihu and Ishaan. Now that the mystery had been uncovered, it only unleashed grief for all of them. Her health was deteriorating fast, and Apurv just hoped she would return before her memories of him were erased.

'I called her a slut, abused her and whatnot. I shouldn't have said such things.' Sia was crying in Ritvik's arms as they sat at their favourite Starbucks outlet.

'You feel guilty, that's enough. Once she is back, don't just apologize. Make her feel good. Knowing that you are dying and still carrying on is not easy. She is a strong girl. She never told anyone about her disease and hid her pain behind a smile. I respect her more now.'

'Isn't it strange? We never even thought this could be the reason she friend-zoned Apurv. No one in school knew about this. She has been going through this for four years, since the time she changed schools.'

Sia felt guilty for the way she had behaved with Amyra. Her conscience was pricking her.

It was then that Apurv walked in and revealed his plan. 'I want you to help me contact Pihu and Ishaan. She wanted to meet them at least once and I want to make her wish come true. Do you have their numbers?'

Sia didn't have their numbers but Apurv's plan uplifted her spirits and she was ready to make it happen. Ritvik too was up for it. The three best friends—Sia, Ritvik and Apurv—had only one goal now: to reunite the three former best friends—Amyra, Pihu and Ishaan.

Sia was scared of messaging Pihu because memories of the bullying and taunting came back to her.

'Will it be right to message her after so long? What will she think about me? Why don't you message her instead?' she asked Apurv.

'No, I won't. You will. Come on, Sia, you don't have to face her in real life. You just need to type and hit send. Put it in a way that she would find hard to refuse.'

'I know but I feel weird. It's been more than two years since we spoke.'

'Two years? You were together till the tenth standard, right? Or did she also leave school like Amyra?'

'No, she was forced to take a gap year and when she repeated the ninth standard, we had already cleared our board exams.'

'Why?'

'Amyra told me one evening before our fallout. It was because of her that Pihu had taken a gap year. Amyra also didn't leave school by choice. She would've been expelled if she didn't, making it hard for her to get admission anywhere else. This is why her dad sought a transfer to another school in Versova.'

'What the fuck are you talking about?'

'Yes, she told me herself. Pihu and Amyra were like sisters, and I had found it strange that she was not even on her Facebook friend list. Amyra told me that she was jealous of Ishaan's and Pihu's closeness. It was out of jealousy that one day at school she stuck bubblegum in Pihu's hair. This was a serious offence and they were called by the principal. Amyra didn't know that Pihu would have to crop her hair short. Pihu took a year off to save herself from the humiliation and Amyra was forced to leave.'

'Was that the reason for her break-up with Ishaan?'

'I think they couldn't handle the distance because they couldn't travel a lot in school. But after that incident, they abused each other and messed up their relationship. It was just a prank that had gone too far. Amyra never imagined that because of her Pihu would have to drop a year. Just because of that guilt she never tried to contact her but she really wanted to apologize. It was not that she didn't try initially, but Pihu didn't respond to her attempts. Ishaan too drifted away when he found out the reason for Amyra's actions. After all, Pihu was his best friend.'

Apurv realized that this situation resembled his life a lot. He encouraged Sia to text Pihu because he knew that even the deepest wounds heal with time. Also, he knew that Pihu wouldn't refuse to meet Amyra once she heard about her condition.

'Send her a message at least. We have to give it a try.'

Sia took a deep breath and opened her Facebook profile to send Pihu a message.

Hey, I hope you remember me from school.
I know we never interacted after you took a

year off but I am sorry to hear about what happened. Amyra told me everything a few days ago because we are in the same college. I hope you are over what happened. Amyra misses you a lot. Her only wish is to meet you and Ishaan once, before her illness takes its toll on her. Yes, you read that right. I want to meet you. Please, don't say no. This is a request. Please reply after reading the message. I am sending you my phone number and will wait for an answer.

After a lot of hesitation, she finally sent the message. They hoped that she would reply soon because they wanted to surprise Amyra when she reached Mumbai.

Hope and expectation were at war. It had been two days and there was no response from Pihu. Sia even commented on her latest picture, asking her to check her inbox. They sent a message to Ishaan as well, but even he had not replied. They had expected something good to happen but now they just felt helpless.

'Do you think this will work?' Sia asked Apurv as they sat in a classroom during the lunch break.

'I don't know. The other option is to contact some other school friend of yours and ask them to get in touch with Pihu and Ishaan.'

'I am sorry but I hardly talked to anyone, and I am not in touch with any classmates. Aren't there any other options?'

'I am afraid not. You don't even know where they stay, so we just have to wait for a reply.'

'Let's wait then.'

Apurv had sent another text to Amyra as he wanted her to see all the messages when she switched on her mobile.

A few years ago, I had totally given up on love. I thought that there was nobody for me. I thought that the ache in my heart would remain with me forever. But then you entered my life and, suddenly, love was real. I crave your love. I crave your smile. I crave the way you look at me. I crave your sweet voice. And I crave you. But we have not talked for a while now, and I'm afraid I'll lose you. I cannot bear thinking of a life without you. I know there is going to come a time—and my heart is telling me it's now—when I'm going to have to say goodbye to you, but I cannot bring myself to do it. I love you and will always be here if you need me. Just don't make me say goodbye.

Apurv had started to lose faith in the supreme power that he believed in. However, a phone call from Sia a few days later restored his faith. Pihu had called Sia and agreed to meet Amyra, but it had taken a lot of convincing. It was after Sia told Pihu about Amyra's condition that she agreed. After all, they had shared so many memories together. No grudge was bigger than a person's life, especially when the person was slowly walking towards the door to death. She told them that Ishaan would join her as well. Whatever the outcome, everyone was up for it.

Amyra knows that she does not have long to live. Still, can she be happy? Why did she build walls around her? Did she fear her friends would break her? Apurv thought.

'Finally, we did it,' Sia said triumphantly.

'I know. Now Amyra will be happy.'

'Seem' is a tricky word because things aren't always exactly as they appear. Amyra may have seemed fine because of the smile on her face, but she was dejected. She felt like a rotten leaf among the fresh blooms of spring. She knew her mom was sad because of her.

In the bleak room with almost no light, Amyra thought about things she knew she should avoid. Her mom gave her hope that she would be fine, but

Amyra knew she was just consoling her. Amyra had accepted her condition, but she was afraid of losing her family and friends. Her heart had cried out in pain when Apurv proposed to her because despite being in love with him, she couldn't say yes. She was losing everything along with her memories. Already she had made him drop her off at her old address in Andheri, where she stayed during her schooldays, which made Apurv search for her there when she went missing. She had also caused him so much trouble after giving him the wrong landmark. She had accidentally told him that she was at the Andheri bus stop when she was in Versova. Her mind used to blank out for certain periods of time, taking her back to the early days of her life. It was during times like these that she felt completely helpless. She had no control over her mind. She had gone through a lot alone because she didn't want to reveal her condition to anyone. But blunders like addressing Apurv as Ishaan made her feel pathetic and so she had considered revealing the truth. That's when her parents took her to the guru they believed in. She had finally decided to tell Apurv, but couldn't do so, making him feel that she had lied to him shamelessly. She still found it difficult to accept that this was the way things were going to be.

The hardest part was accepting that they could never be together. Each day with Alzheimer's was a struggle and, in an attempt to hide it, she had lost her friends. When she had visited the guru last week, she had wished for a meeting with Pihu and Ishaan because she knew time was running out. She wished Apurv and Sia would share the same bond as before. Her to-do list was fast turning into a should-have-done list.

But I Still Love You

I'm breaking
And I can't be fixed
I'm missing
But will I be missed?

I can't let you in,
So don't come near
I'm fighting a battle
That I'll never win.

So what's the point
of continuing to fight?
When my restless days
Turn into restless nights

This life hasn't been fair
What was God's cause?
Why did He put me on this earth?
Was I born just to die?

I'm losing sight
Of what I've already seen
I'm losing my grip,
And I'm barely seventeen.

Amyra was typing on her mobile when she heard a familiar voice. She was in a hospital bed with her arm injected with IVs to counter the weakness brought on by the mental stress. The doctors had given up on her mental state but were fighting for her physical well-being.

'Amyra, I am here.' Apurv entered the room and greeted her sister and parents. She stared at him with a blank face. Ritvik and Sia followed him. Amyra smiled at Sia. Apurv sensed that she was still upset about what had happened that day and was ignoring him. He wanted to confess his love for her, despite her parents sitting right there. *I love her, I just love her.* His heart ached looking at her. *I hate you, God, I will never forgive you. If you were human, I would have dragged you to the highest court of humanity to prove that your decision to take Amyra's life is wrong.*

'How are you? I am not well.' Amyra sighed, still ignoring Apurv.

Sia didn't react while Ritvik inquired, 'Aren't you feeling a little better?'

Amyra didn't reply and turned towards Sia instead.

Sia looked at Amyra. 'We have a surprise for you, and I am sure it'll make you feel better.'

'Really? Can you take this pain away?'

'Yes.' Sia beckoned Ishaan and Pihu to step in.

'Friendship is the only gift we can give you,' said Apurv.

Amyra couldn't believe that her wish was coming true.

'Sia?' Amyra asked in shock, ignoring Apurv once again.

Sia held her hand and assured her that this was really happening. None of them said anything but their eyes expressed all their emotions. Pihu sat beside her and touched her cheek gently. The dry flames inside Amyra's cold heart burnt so bright that they melted the toughest stone of ire that Pihu carried within her. It didn't take even a single word for them to feel the connection they once shared.

'I am sorry. I didn't want to hurt you,' Amyra cried.

'I know. But we both moved on to our new lives so quickly that we completely forgot how important we were to each other.' Pihu's eyes were filled with tears.

'I shifted to Versova this year.'

For a second, Pihu couldn't comprehend what she meant because she thought Amyra had moved almost three years ago when they were in the ninth standard. But Pihu ignored this and hugged Amyra tightly. Ishaan stood back, his eyes moist. When Amyra looked at him, he slowly moved forward and, keeping in mind her parents, sat beside her as if he were just a close school friend. However, her parents seemed to understand and stepped outside to give them some privacy. 'You are still special to me,' Ishaan said while caressing her forehead.

This made Apurv feel uncomfortable, but he knew that Amyra's feelings mattered more. He wanted to leave the room, but he knew she would feel bad. Also, it had been his decision to reunite them. But he was completely taken aback when Amyra said, 'Can you kiss me?'

'Now?' Ishaan looked around the room.

'Yes, please.'

Ishaan gazed at Apurv in confusion, not knowing what to do.

'Please,' Amyra begged again.

Ishaan gave her a small peck on the cheek and smiled. Apurv opened his eyes only after he heard Amyra's mother whispering to the doctor who had arrived to conduct a routine check-up. Ishaan and Pihu left after a while. It was then that Apurv finally spoke to Amyra. 'This was your only wish, right? To meet

Ishaan and Pihu? I had promised myself that I would do anything to fulfil your . . .' He stopped himself from saying the words 'last wish'. Instead, he said, 'I would do anything to see you smile. I love you.'

He hoped to hear her say that she loved him too. But Amyra gave him a confused look. 'You love me?'

'Why are you acting like you don't know me? I know you love me too.' Apurv smiled as he moved closer to her.

'I don't love you. I don't even know you.' Amyra's words broke his heart. His biggest fear had come true. The eraser in her head had already removed Apurv and all their memories from her mind. Now he understood why she had stared at him with a blank expression when he entered. She remembered Sia because she had known her since school.

'Now I know why she said they shifted to Versova this year.' Apurv told the others.

'Why?'

'My role in her life is over. It's time for me to pack up.'

Still, he refused to let go. The nurse brought coffee for her and placed it on the table. The scene reminded Apurv of their first meeting, and he snatched the coffee away to take a sip, burning his tongue in the process. 'Excuse me, that's mine.'

The words were the same. Back then, they had been strangers. And now, after so many days together, they were strangers again. He was ready to relive every moment with her, but time separated them. He was moving ahead in time while she was moving backwards.

Three months later:

I honestly feel like I'm losing my mind. As time keeps passing, I'm falling behind. The world seems unclear to me. The best of me is gone and I do not want to remember it. Don't try to make me understand, let me just rest and know you are with me, Mom. It started so simply, just a phrase here and there or maybe a memory that vanished into thin air. I started to repeat it over and over again. Slowly, it grew worse as the seasons passed by. It's such a task to even go anywhere. For the last three months, I have immersed myself in a routine. Alarms, voice messages and reminders are my only partners. There are photographs pinned all over my room to keep me from forgetting the people who matter. But I still do. At times, it seems like I have two diseases—Alzheimer's and the knowledge of Alzheimer's. When I wander, don't tell me to come and sit down; instead wander with me. When I call for my grandmother, don't tell me she died, Mom; reassure me, cuddle me and tell me about her. When I get angry, please don't reach for the drugs, but try to understand what I'm saying. If I don't eat or drink, it may be because I've forgotten how to; show me what to do. Mom, will there really be a day when I won't be able to recognize you? How could I not, Mom? I don't mind losing everyone else, but what will I do without you?

It's not always hearts, sometimes even minds break. Amyra needed time but, slowly and surely, the disease was coming down on her. Everyone around her said she had changed, that she wasn't the same. Her mom bathed her, dressed her and loved her. The nurses told them that she would go back to her childhood and act like she was five. But if we could, how many of us would love to be five again? So maybe being five again wasn't so bad after all.

Her friends, including Apurv, proved the doctors wrong as they still cared for her like before. Over the past three months she had looked at Apurv as a stranger, but for him she was the same Amyra. He had to rewrite the college play at the last moment, but their biggest problem was the uncertainty over the leading lady. However, Apurv and Ritvik both convinced Sia to take up the role, and she finally accepted. The play was a hit. All the delegates not only appreciated Sia's performance but even the clothes she had designed for all the characters. Even her parents had big smiles on their faces. But it was performing publicly for the first time that completely changed Sia's outlook on life. She had acquired a new confidence. She didn't feel insecure about her appearance any more. Apurv had even written a play on Amyra's life, one in which he wanted Sia to play the lead. One person certainly can change your perceptions. Where he used his writing to make girls fall in love with him, his first play ended up being about a girl he loved more than anything else.

Please say my name, just once today. Tell me you remember who I am, please just whisper softly. Don't let this be the day when you look past my face. We can't let go, there are many more things we have to do, many more walks to take and many more memories to make. Apurv's inner voice screamed as he stood in front of Amyra in her room.

'It's your birthday month. What gift do you want? Remember, we planned to celebrate it together this time.'

Amyra shook her head, unable to recollect as she looked towards the sticky note on which the month was written. *April 2017.*

Amyra looked back at Apurv and smiled with the same elegance that was characteristic of her.

'Even though I can't remember who you are, your presence makes me happy. I wish to relive all our moments together. I'm sure you were my favourite person.'

Her words eased his restless soul and mended his aching heart. The emotions he felt for Amyra were irreplaceable regardless of whether she was his friend or girlfriend. 'I love you, Amyra.'

'I love you too.' Amyra smiled. She loved him for the care he showed and effort he took to make her smile.

Although he knew that it wasn't the same as before, she still sent butterflies fluttering in his stomach.

The next day, when Apurv was in college, he got a call from Amyra's sister.

'Apurv?' she sounded breathless.

'Yes, Nivi. What happened?'

'Apurv, Didi is no more. Please come fast.'

It felt like the world had stopped around him. Although he had known that he would have to face this eventuality, he wasn't prepared. You can never prepare yourself for such moments. She had left him all alone.

Apurv was sitting with Ritvik and Sia when the call came.

'She didn't recognize you again?' asked Sia.

'She didn't talk to me and will never talk to me again.'

'Why? Who called?'

'Amyra is no more.'

I love you too. Those were her last words to him. If Apurv knew that those would be her last words, he wouldn't have minded being 'just friends' with her. Apurv rushed to her house with teary eyes and a heavy heart. His body went cold when he saw her lying lifeless, covered in a white sheet. The moment he entered, Nivi ran to him and hugged him. His chest felt tight and he could barely breathe.

He remembered Amyra's words. 'Till there is life, there will be struggle; till there is struggle, there will be life.'

Her soul had left and her struggle with life had ended. They hadn't had a chance to say goodbye. Their love story would remain an unfinished book.

A few weeks later, Nivi found a note in Amyra's wardrobe with Apurv's name on it. Without any delay, she handed it over to him.

I am afraid I won't ever gather the courage to give this to you. It's so funny how everything in this life can seem so small when you look death in the eye. We live our entire lives trying to achieve useless goals, when in reality they don't matter. Live in the moment, live now and be happy. Go lie under the stars and listen to the songs of the universe. The stars have been around for far longer than us and will exist even when we cease to. I'll be looking at you, Apurv, from above, reminding you that till there is life there will be struggle; and till there is struggle, there will be life. Stop wasting time worrying about things that don't matter and just enjoy life. Find yourself, chase your dreams and smile. Be happy, be free and be yourself, for that is all you can be. Don't shed a tear because I am gone; smile because we got to spend time together. Tell Ritvik and Sia to be happy and have at least a dozen kids.

The letter brought a smile to his face. Apurv was lucky that he had two friends who constantly supported him while he mourned for Amyra. They tried to cheer him up by taking him to watch movies and to restaurants. Despite being a couple, they included him in all their plans.

Apurv decided to turn his back on yesterday and to live for tomorrow. He didn't just remember Amyra as a sad memory, he cherished every moment spent with her and let it live on.